# RANGO

## THE NOVEL

*By*
**JUSTINE *and* RON FONTES**

*Based on the screenplay written by*
**JOHN LOGAN**

*Story by*
**JOHN LOGAN,**
**GORE VERBINSKI,**
*and* **JAMES WARD BYRKIT**

STERLING

New York / London
www.sterlingpublishing.com/kids

STERLING and the distinctive Sterling logo are registered trademarks of
Sterling Publishing Co., Inc.

**Library of Congress Cataloging-in-Publication Data Available**

Lot #:
2  4  6  8  10  9  7  5  3  1
12/10
Published by Sterling Publishing Co., Inc.
387 Park Avenue South, New York, NY 10016
TM & © 2011 Paramount Pictures. All Rights Reserved.
Distributed in Canada by Sterling Publishing
C/o Canadian Manda Group, 165 Dufferin Street
Toronto, Ontario, Canada M6K 3H6
Distributed in the United Kingdom by GMC Distribution Services
Castle Place, 166 High Street, Lewes, East Sussex, England BN7 1XU
Distributed in Australia by Capricorn Link (Australia) Pty. Ltd.
P.O. Box 704, Windsor, NSW 2756, Australia

Sterling ISBN 978-1-4027-8443-9

For information about custom editions, special sales, premium and
corporate purchases, please contact Sterling Special Sales
Department at 800-805-5489 or specialsales@sterlingpublishing.com.

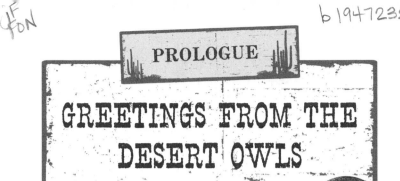

# PROLOGUE

# GREETINGS FROM THE DESERT OWLS

"GREETINGS, GENTLE READERS and lovers of fine Mexican cuisine! We are the Mariachis: Chico on trumpet, Raoul on the guitar, Lupe on violin, and yours truly, Señor Flan, on accordion.

"Today we honor, in song and story, the life of a great legend. This is the tale of a chameleon who discovered his true identity by becoming a hero.

*"How is that possible?"* you might wonder. Turn the page and find out. Go ahead. Don't be shy. How else will you discover the legend of the lonely lizard known as Rango?"

# CHAPTER 1

# WHO AM I?

**MOST HEROES** don't start life in a glass box. But Rango wasn't a typical hero. He was a pet chameleon who lived in a terrarium. His only companions in captivity were a headless, legless, one-armed doll; a windup fish named Mr. Timms; a plastic palm tree; and a dead bug called Dr. Marx.

Rango considered himself an actor with a vivid imagination, and with it, he invented all kinds of plays to perform with his co-stars.

Using palm fronds as curtains, the lonely lizard began his latest show. "The stage is set; the night moist with apprehension. Alone in her chamber, the princess prepares to meet her destiny."

In his highest-pitched, most feminine squeak, Rango recited the doll's line, "It is far better to nourish

worms than to live without love."

Rango continued his dramatic narration and pushed a glass toward the doll's hand. "She reaches for the poison chalice. Meanwhile, the wicked Malvolio plots his ascension to the throne."

With a quick cue to Mr. Timms, who played the part of the evil Malvolio, Rango let out a cruel, villainous laugh.

Hiding behind Victor, the palm tree, Rango announced, "Hark! Who goes there?"

As imaginary trumpets blared, Rango switched parts again and bounded onto center stage. "'Tis I, the much anticipated hero, returning to rescue his emotionally unstable maiden."

Rango rushed toward the pool where the chameleon, playing the part of Mr. Timms, continued to cackle.

He raised a plastic hors d'oeuvre pick like a shining sword and threatened, "Unhand her, you jailers of virtue! Or taste the bitter sting of my vengeance! The sting of my . . ."

Rango stopped the show. Somehow even his mighty imagination had stalled. He turned to his co-stars.

"What's that, Victor?" Rango carried on an imaginary conversation with the palm tree. "My character is

undefined? That's absurd. I know who I am. I'm the . . .
the guy . . . the protagonist, the hero. Every story needs
a hero. I mean, who else is better qualified to bask in the
adulation of his numerous companions . . ."

But the lonely lizard's voice trailed off in mid-
sentence, fading almost as fast as his smile. Pretending
could only get him so far. Who was he, really?

Rango walked slowly toward the nearest wall. He
breathed on the glass and then drew a frame around his
face in the fog. Rango murmured, "The stage is waiting.
The audience thirsts for adventure . . . Who am I? I could
be anyone . . ."

Suddenly, the chameleon sprang into action. "I could
be a sea captain returning from a mighty voyage. Or I
could be a rogue anthropologist, battling pythons down
in the Congo! Down, Chongo! Down!" he exclaimed as
he fought his own tail.

"That's it—conflict!" Rango announced. "Victor, you
were right. I have been undefined."

Rango raised his glass in a toast, "The hero cannot
exist in a vacuum. What our story needs is an ironic,
unexpected event that will propel the hero into
conflict . . ."

Just as Rango spoke those very words, a car horn blared from above. HONK! HONK! *SCREECH!*

Rango's terrarium, which had been in the back of a station wagon speeding down a stretch of highway crossing the mighty Mojave Desert, was suddenly thrust into the air.

The confused chameleon watched as his terrarium flew out the wagon's open back window in slow motion.

The glass box landed on the hard pavement, shattering instantly. Rango fell on a shard of glass that slid across the hot asphalt.

The lizard looked up just in time to see the station wagon speed away, getting smaller and smaller until it became just a speck on the horizon.

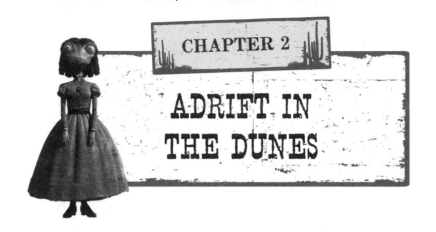

## CHAPTER 2

# ADRIFT IN THE DUNES

RANGO WALKED OVER to Mr. Timms and assessed the damage. The windup fish flapped in a puddle that was quickly evaporating under the blazing sun.

"Oye!" a voice called from nearby.

Startled, Rango looked around. There was something on the road.

"That's right. I'm talking to you," the voice continued. "Don't be shy. Come. It's okay . . ."

Rango followed the voice a short distance down the highway. Double black skid marks from the station wagon led him to an armadillo with tire tracks across his flattened belly. This half-squashed creature was appropriately called Roadkill.

"That's it. A little closer," Roadkill urged. "I won't bite you. I just need a little help here."

Rango thought the armadillo looked beyond help. "Uh . . . are you okay?" he asked, not sure he really wanted to hear the answer.

"I must get to the other side," Roadkill asserted. "This is my quest. The Spirit of the West waits for me, amigo. They say he rides an alabaster carriage with golden guardians to protect him—"

"What are you talking about?" Rango interrupted, confused by the strange creature and his even stranger ideas.

"Enlightenment," Roadkill declared. "We are nothing without it."

"Look, I need water—hydration. My lips are chapped. I need some lotion. I'm down to one layer of skin already. Pretty soon I'm going to start seeing my insides . . . sort of like, uh, what you've got going there," he said and pointed to the smushed armadillo.

Rango looked away from the strange spectacle. All he could see for miles in all directions was sand, highway, and more sweltering sand.

"Listen, I can't survive in the desert, okay? I don't belong here," he pleaded, wondering what a squashed armadillo could do to fix the situation.

9

Could he trust this peculiar stranger? Did he have a choice?

ZOOM! A truck suddenly rushed over the exact spot where Rango had just stood. The wind in its wake lifted the lizard right off the ground. Then more speeding vehicles sent the hapless chameleon careening from mud flaps to antennas, pavement to windshield, until he finally landed in a cloud of dust at Roadkill's feet.

"The path to knowledge is fraught with consequence," Roadkill observed.

"Yeah . . . I'm just looking for the path to water," Rango said. After bouncing off all those hot, dusty cars he was even thirstier than before.

"If you want to find water, you must first find Dirt," Roadkill explained. "Destiny, she is kind to you. Tomorrow is Wednesday. The water comes. At noon the townspeople gather for a mysterious ritual."

At the thought of finding a town amid all this nothingness, Rango's hopes lifted. He stood up and brushed himself off. "A town? You mean with real people and everything? Where?"

Roadkill lifted his wooden staff and pointed across the sands. "A day's journey. Follow your shadow."

Rango looked out across the barren dunes. "You want me to just walk out into the desert?"

"That is the way," Roadkill assured him.

"Okay, then I'm going," Rango announced, hoping that the armadillo would somehow spring up and show him the way. "I am leaving the road now. I am walking into the desert . . . alone."

As soon as his foot left the hot pavement, Rango felt the burn of the Mojave's sun-baked sand. He had never experienced anything like this in his terrarium.

Rango lifted his other foot, and then cautiously dropped it to the pale sand. He could practically hear the sole sizzle!

"We all have our journeys to make. I will see you on the other side," Roadkill concluded.

And with that, Rango headed off, alone once more.

⋆ ⋆ ⋆

As Rango made his way across the barren desert, the owl mariachi band commented on the chameleon's tale of woe from a faraway limb of a cactus.

"Here in the Mojave Desert, animals have had millions of years to adapt to the harsh environment. But the lizard? He is going to die."

That same thought crossed Rango's mind several times as he stumbled in the unbearable heat. The sun scorched his sensitive skin, and his limbs felt as heavy as lead.

"Don't move," a voice commanded suddenly.

Rango froze. "What?"

He looked around and saw nothing except a cactus, rocks, and, of course, sand, sand, and more sand!

Thinking he must be losing his mind, Rango took another step.

The voice repeated urgently, "Don't move!"

"Not moving!" Rango froze, even though he still didn't know who he was talking to.

"Try to blend in," the mysterious voice instructed.

"Huh? Blend in? What do you mean?" Rango wondered if the heat had boiled his brain. Who was talking to him?

He stared at a rock from which the bossy voice seemed to emanate. Suddenly, the "rock" opened one eye and commanded again, "Blend in!"

Rango blinked one round lizard eye, and then the other. Even staring right at the stone-colored frog known as Rock-Eye, he found it extremely hard to distinguish

the strange creature from an actual rock.

A large, looming shadow suddenly sped over the hot sand. The shadow belonged to a huge red-tailed hawk that zoomed through the air high above the parched, baking lizard.

"Too late," Rock-Eye reported.

The chameleon panicked. "No, no. It's not too late! I'm blending. I'm a blender!"

Rango froze with his arms bent to look like the branches of a cactus. The little lizard had never seen such a big and ferocious-looking bird before. When the hawk came in close, the wind off its powerful wing-beats tickled his skin.

Rango couldn't help himself. He screamed! The terrified chameleon's skin suddenly changed from dull green to hot pink, turquoise, and all kinds of crazy colors.

The hawk began its deadly dive.

"Oh no, here he comes," the frog warned. "Now, you run!"

Rango saw the hawk's penetrating eyes and the sharp points of its terrifying talons getting closer and closer. There was no question about it. It was time to run!

Fleeing over the burning sand, he frantically searched for a place to hide from the hawk. At the last second, Rango spotted an empty soda bottle and scrambled inside.

The hawk approached the bottle, pecking and snapping at the glass with its vicious curved beak.

"Whoa . . . testy," Rango remarked from the safety of his new glass cage.

It was almost like being back in his terrarium—until the hawk wrapped his talons around the bottle and took off! In seconds, Rango dangled high above the desert floor. With every wing beat, the rocks and cactus groves grew smaller and smaller.

"No, please, no, please!" Rango begged, adding, "I'm afraid of heights . . . no-no-NO!"

Abruptly, the hawk released the bottle from his grip. Rango held his breath as his fragile shelter plummeted toward the fast-approaching desert below. Rango's eyes swiveled in different directions. He braced for impact— and perhaps death.

BOING! The bottle bounced off a rock and didn't break. That's because it wasn't a rock at all. It was Rock-Eye.

A speeding shadow flitted across the sand. Rango recognized the hawk's silhouette against the sky as the bird of prey zoomed toward them again. Pushing frantically on one side, Rango rolled the bottle away from the attacking hawk.

THUNK! CRASH! Rango's bottle hit a rock and broke! Rock-Eye ran up, laughing at Rango's misfortune.

Then with a terrifying SWOOP the hawk suddenly snatched Rock-Eye and flew off with him kicking desperately in his claws!

Out of danger for the moment, Rango walked until the sun finally sank. Exhausted and thirstier than he had ever been in his whole life, he climbed into a broken drainpipe and fell into a deep, nightmare-filled sleep.

**WHOOSH!** A tidal wave of water flushed a sleeping Rango out of the drainpipe. He slammed down on the sand with a dull thud. The precious liquid vanished almost as soon as it left the pipe, sinking into the grains and evaporating into the hot, dry air.

A boot impatiently tapped the sand near Rango's face. The lizard looked up from the boot, right into the fierce gaze of a pretty rancher lizard.

"Get your slimy, webbed phalanges off my boots!" Beans demanded.

"Oh . . . sorry," Rango apologized.

"I got a bead on you, stranger. So get up real slow . . . unless you want to spend the better part of the afternoon puttin' your face back together!" the cowgirl threatened.

Rango stood up slowly with his hands raised.

"Who are you?" the cowgirl asked.

"Who am I?" Rango echoed.

"I'm asking the questions here!" she shouted. "Our town is drying up. We're in the middle of a drought. Now someone is dumping water in the desert. It's a puzzle of undeterminable size and dimension, but I intend to find out what role you play in all this."

The frightened chameleon grasped at the one familiar word and prattled on about his latest acting projects.

"You ain't from around here, are you?" the rancher observed, walking to her wagon full of empty bottles.

"What's your name?" Rango asked.

The pretty lizard replied with one word: "Beans."

"That's a funny kind of name," Rango observed. For someone so pretty, he had imagined something like Annabelle or Evangeline.

"What can I say? My daddy plum loved baked beans." Beans shrugged and carried on about her father, but then stopped abruptly mid-rant, frozen solid as a TV dinner. Rango had never seen anything like it.

"Beans . . . Miss Beans? . . . Hello?" He whistled, but the pretty lizard remained as still as a statue. "Hello?"

Rango waved his hand in front of her face. Beans did not even blink. Rango put his arm around her shoulder, and in a few seconds Beans continued talking as if nothing had happened.

Beans suddenly noticed Rango's arm on her shoulder. "What are you doing?"

Rango defended himself, "You were frozen."

Embarrassed, Beans sighed. "It's a defense mechanism. Actually, lots of lizards have it."

Rango was skeptical. "You're making that up."

Beans didn't care whether the stranger believed her or not. She had supplies to buy, a mystery to solve, and a vital appointment at noon. The cowgirl climbed into the wagon and asked, "So, you gonna die out here or you want a ride into town?"

The thought of being left alone to die in the desert terrified Rango beyond words.

"No-no-no, I mean yeah . . . no . . . yes, please . . ." he stammered, clumsily climbing up into the wagon beside Beans. After bumping her knees and generally making a nuisance of himself, Rango finally sat down, adding, "Thank you. Sorry."

With a flick of the reins, the wagon rumbled across

the Mojave. Giant plumes of dust rose up behind the wheels. Rango coughed. How he longed for a cool drink of water!

Rango spent the trip talking about his favorite subject, which was of course himself, until Beans stopped the wagon and announced, "Well, here we are."

In the distance, Rango saw a cluster of sagging buildings. Dropping to the sand, he said, "Well, I sure do appreciate this, Miss Beans. And if there's ever anything I could . . ."

The cowgirl had no time for more fancy speeches. "Yah!" she said with a snap of the reins. The wagon clattered off before Rango could finish.

After a hot, dry walk across yet more blistering sand, Rango finally saw an old, wooden sign at the edge of the clump of clapboard firetraps. It read: Welcome to Dirt.

Roadkill had promised Rango a town and civilization, but Dirt was none of that. Instead, it was a dusty little dump that seemed like the capital of despair. Rango walked on, scanning the storefronts for water.

On Main Street, two miserable farmer critters discussed the drought that Beans had mentioned.

"Well, we gave it our best shot, but had to sell out. Can't grow no crops without no water . . ."

Further along Main Street, Rango saw two tall structures: a big clock tower and a water tower anchored to the ground with ropes.

At the sight of the second tower, Rango swallowed painfully and his heart fluttered with happy anticipation. A water tower must be full of water, right? Soon, soon, the dried-out lizard would have WATER!

BAM!

A rock hit Rango on the side of the head. He turned and saw a group of scruffy kids snickering.

The stranger's angry stare sent them all scattering, except for one dainty aye-aye in an old-fashioned pinafore. To his surprise, Rango realized this sweet little opossum girl carried a slingshot.

"OW!" he complained loudly as another rock hit him squarely on the head. "What was that for?"

"You're funny-looking," Priscilla replied.

"Oh, yeah? You're funny-looking, too," Rango razzed her right back.

Priscilla was not about to be outdone. "That's a funny-looking shirt."

"That's a funny-looking dress," Rango countered.

"You got funny-looking eyes," Priscilla went on, undaunted.

The chameleon blinked both lizard eyes. One stared at the girl, and the other wandered up and down Main Street.

Rango couldn't let Priscilla have the last word, so he taunted on, "You got a funny-looking face!"

"You're a stranger. Strangers don't last long here," Priscilla concluded, and walked away.

Rango spotted Beans down the street at the general store. The cowgirl had just loaded her wagon with supplies with help from the storekeeper, Mr. Furgus.

"Here are your beans, Beans," said the old white bird.

"I'm gonna need some more feed, too," she replied.

But the storekeeper shook his head. "Now Beans, you owe me three quarts already. I can't give you more credit."

"But I'll have what I owe you at noon," Beans protested.

"You don't understand," Mr. Fergus began. "It's not me. It's Mr. Merrimack down at the bank. He cut off all credit."

By this point in the conversation the desperately thirsty chameleon had almost reached the store. Rango waved and shouted, "Hey, Beans! BEANS!"

The cowgirl didn't react. Surely she could hear him from this short distance.

Rango called again, "Miss Beans!"

Mr. Furgus squinted at the approaching stranger. "You know that there feller?"

Rango kept calling, "Hey, Miss Beans!"

But even as he spoke her name, Beans coolly assured the storekeeper, "Nope." Then she went inside the store.

Rango decided the thing to do was to blend in. He watched some men pass him along the dusty street. He tried to copy each one's odd walk, but he just couldn't get the motions right.

Finally, he saw a porcupine named Mr. Snuggles who sauntered by with a classic cowboy swagger. Rango copied it exactly. He had found his Western walk!

Rango swaggered over to the saloon. The honky-tonk piano tinkled loudly as he boldly pushed open the swinging double doors. The thirsty chameleon could practically taste a big, cool glass of ice water.

As soon as the doors flapped shut behind the

newcomer, the music stopped. Every eye in the joint turned to stare at the lizard approaching the bar.

Rango's walk was perfect! Everything in his manner seemed authentic. You could practically smell the saddle soap on him. Then he said, "I'd like a glass of water."

For a moment, the crowded room remained silent. Then everyone burst out laughing!

A tough-looking mole named Hazel Moats cackled, "He wants a glass of water!"

"Give'm the spittoon!" someone suggested.

"Cactus juice. That's what we got," said Buford, the bullfrog behind the counter. Buford slid a bottle down to the thirsty lizard.

Rango laughed nervously and then swallowed a shot of the fiery liquid. The pampered pet had never tasted anything like this. His eyeballs rattled. His lips puckered uncontrollably, and finally his butt cheeks exploded in a loud FART!

A stinky old mouse named Spoons stroked his long white beard and said, "Hey there, fruit cup. You're a long way from home, ain't ya? Who exactly are you?"

Rango looked at his reflection in the mirror behind the bar, contemplating the question he had so often asked

himself in his terrarium. "Who am I?" Rango mused. "I could be anyone."

Then he looked down at the cactus juice bottle. The label said "Hecho en Durango." Rango slid his thumb over part of the label and read RANGO.

"What's the matter? You missing your mommy's mangos?" Spoons taunted impatiently.

The chameleon's eyes narrowed. His voice dropped into a low and manly Western drawl. "As a matter of fact I am." The lizard spun around to stare straight at Spoons. "But not as much as your daddy's cookin'!"

Spoons jumped. The stinky old mouse hadn't expected the skinny stranger to be so defiant. "Exactly where did you say you were from?"

"Me? I'm from the West . . . out there, beyond the horizon . . . past the sunset . . . THE FAR WEST," replied the chameleon. He strutted around the room, adding, "Yeah, that's right, hombres."

The lizard took a toothpick out of one of the customer's mouths. Rango chewed on the pick in a cool, nonchalant way. Then he took Hazel's fancy hat and put it on before swaggering over to the poker game.

"I seen things make a grown man lose control of his

glandular functions," the lizard bragged. "You spend three days in a horse carcass living off your own juices . . . it'll change a man. Oh, yeah."

Rango grabbed the deck of cards and shuffled it dramatically. But his shuffling wasn't nearly as expert as his bragging, and the cards flew everywhere.

Rango quickly covered his error, "Got a few extra aces in this deck, gents. Just the way I like it."

He strutted back to Spoons, concluding, "So, no, my little rodent friend, I am not from around these parts. You might say I'm from everywhere there's trouble brewing."

The chameleon drained a shot of cactus juice. This time the fiery brew went down without any problem. Then he declared, "Name's . . . Rango."

This exciting new name sped around the saloon in whispers, murmurs, and gasps. And so the legend was born.

One of the regulars, a cat named Elbows, asked, "Hey, are you the fella that killed them Jenkins brothers?"

"Mmhmm," Rango replied. "With one bullet. Don't get no deader."

Elbows' feline pal, Elgin, didn't see how that could be possible. "All seven of them?"

Rango felt trapped in his own fib, but since the whole bar waited for his answer, he simply made the lie even bigger. "That's right. All seven of them."

A jittery toad named Waffles wondered, "Exactly how'd you do that, Mr. Rango?"

Everyone gathered round to hear the lying lizard's explanation.

"You know I'm glad you asked me that," Rango fibbed. "And I will be happy to tell you how . . ." The chameleon stalled while his imagination constructed a tall tale worthy of Davy Crockett and Calamity Jane.

\* \* \*

While Rango was busy spinning his story, Beans was on her way to the bank to ask Mr. Merrimack why she couldn't buy more feed on credit.

When she arrived, Parsons, the teller, was standing behind his cage measuring out some water. Parsons poured the precious liquid slowly and precisely.

In Dirt, water was money. Gold, silver, and pictures of dead presidents don't mean much if you're thirsty in the desert. So the town traded in the one thing everyone always needed: water.

Beans marched straight into the banker's office.

26

Daddy's problems had forced the cowgirl to learn to take care of herself. Today that meant finding out why Dirt was running out of water—and how to get the pints she needed for that feed!

Beans watched as Mr. Merrimack dropped two stomach settling tablets into an empty glass. Without any water, the tablets couldn't fizz. But the worried banker stirred the glass anyway.

Then the beaver tried to explain to the gritty cowgirl why he couldn't loan her the water she needed to hang onto her daddy's land. Ever since the drought began, Mr. Merrimack had given similar bad news to lots of folks in Dirt. Lately things had gotten even worse.

The chubby banker's spoon bounced against the sides of his glass, crushing the tablets. "I don't rightly have a choice, Beans. Times are hard. We just can't give any more credit."

Mr. Merrimack crunched the chalky tablets, which fizzed briefly on his thirsty tongue.

Beans could not accept Mr. Merrimack's excuses. "But this here is the bank. This is where you keep the water!"

Mr. Merrimack laughed nervously, and then suddenly

became serious. "Beans, you've been like a niece to me ever since your daddy . . . did *not* fall drunk down a mine shaft. And I've tried to protect you and others from certain . . . realities . . . oh, and uh . . . the weight of the realities are bearing down . . ."

Beans interrupted, fearing the old banker might have a stroke. "Mr. Merrimack . . . are you alright?"

The banker took a deep breath. "Beans, I need to show you something."

Beans had never been so close to the vault before. The safe was an old glass-fronted washing machine with a big lock on the door. Inside sat a large bottle holding the town's water supply.

Beans stared at the almost empty bottle and gasped, "That's all that's left?!"

Mr. Merrimack sighed. "And this is the reserve! I don't know if you've noticed but folks just aren't making deposits anymore."

Fear ran through Bean's brain. She looked around the vault frantically. Cowgirls don't give up, but what could she do?

"Mr. Merrimack, if I don't get some water, I'm going to lose my ranch. And you're telling me this is all that's

left in the whole town?! Now that just doesn't make any cotton-picking sense!"

Beans almost froze but managed to continue. "Now, listen. Someone is dumping water in the desert. I've seen it with my own eyes."

Mr. Merrimack ushered her out of the vault, and then closed and locked the door. "Well, we can all dream, but this is the reality," the banker stated miserably. "Why do you think so many people are selling out? They just can't make it."

"Well what do you expect me to do?" Beans demanded. She already owed two quarts to the grocer, but how could she pay him without feed for her stock?

Mr. Merrimack said, "I suppose we could talk to the mayor. I hear he's been helping out people in this time of crisis."

"The mayor?" Beans wondered what kind of help that tricky old tortoise could be offering.

"He may be our only hope," Mr. Merrimack concluded glumly.

Back at the saloon, Rango was winding up as well. He stood on the bar, surrounded by awestruck listeners, reciting the exciting climax of how he killed all seven

Jenkins brothers. Everyone cheered and ordered more rounds of cactus juice!

But before Buford could even pour one more glass, Bad Bill, a hideous Gila monster, burst through the double doors, followed closely by his gang: Chorizo, who was ugly even for a rat, and two twitchy rabbits, Stump and Kinski, who were a combination of dangerous and deranged.

The bully picked on the first critter he saw—until he noticed Rango surrounded by his adoring audience. Bad Bill liked to turn strangers into new victims.

He stared at the skinny chameleon who stared back at him. Bill continued toward Rango who gulped drily. The fiery cactus juice had done nothing to slake his awful thirst.

Spoons spoke up. "You know who that is, Bill? That there is Rango!" the stinky mouse declared.

Waffles jumped in, "Yeah, he's not afraid of you."

Other patrons chimed in, emboldened by Waffles' defiant speech.

Bad Bill didn't like the sound of this. He plucked the nasty cigar butt from Buford's mouth. Everyone watched as the bully took a puff, and then blew smoke right in Rango's face!

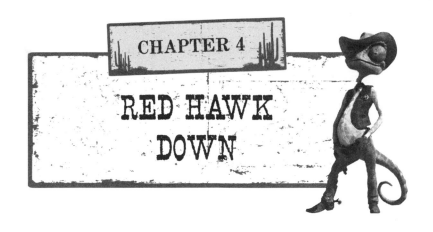

## CHAPTER 4

# RED HAWK DOWN

**THE CROWD** *ooh*ed with excitement.

Without thinking, Rango did something bold, wild, and thoroughly unexpected. He seized the cigar butt and swallowed it!

The crowd *aaah*ed in amazement. They thought Rango was tough!

But the chameleon was neither tough nor fireproof. Rango's eyes clouded with smoke. He gestured frantically for cactus juice.

Buford poured a generous shot. Rango threw the spicy liquid down his burning throat. For a moment, the chameleon seemed fine. Then suddenly, Rango burped fire right in Bad Bill's face!

WHOOM! The Gila monster's ugly mug vanished behind a bright blast of flames. When the smoke cleared,

Bad Bill's eyebrows continued to sizzle.

Rango grabbed a towel and tried to slap out the flames, but ended up hitting Bill in the face and making the fire even bigger. Frantic, Rango reached for the nearest cup of liquid and splashed it all over Bad Bill's face.

WHOOSH! Rango gasped in horror as cactus juice ignited more brilliant flames. He kept trying to smother the flames until Bill's face no longer smoldered. Soot made the Gila monster's face even blacker than usual. His eyebrows were completely gone!

Rango sighed. "There . . . all better."

BAM! Before the startled chameleon quite knew what was happening, Bad Bill challenged him to a showdown. Would the lizard accept the dare—or chicken out?

★ ★ ★

Bad Bill and his boys stood at one end of Main Street and Rango stood at the other.

"Whoa! Time out," the scared chameleon stalled. "Alright, now. I'm gonna give you fellas one last chance to reconsider."

Suddenly, the sky turned black as the shadow of the ferocious Red-Tailed Hawk darkened the dust of Main Street.

Rango bluffed on, "Um . . . Ah . . . If you don't want to reconsider, I might consider reconsidering myself."

The hawk swooped closer. Preoccupied with talking his way out of the duel, Rango still did not notice the scary shadow of the huge bird.

But Bad Bill and the other townsfolk saw the hawk! All up and down the shabby street, shutters slammed shut while frightened folks ducked behind closed doors. Stump and Kinski scrambled for shelter, leaving their leader standing frozen—as still as Beans—in his tracks in the middle of the street.

It only took another second, and the bully ran for his life!

Delighted by this unexpected turn of events, Rango exalted, "Now that is what I'm talking about. Things are going to be different around here now that Rango's in town."

The hawk landed quietly behind the chameleon, who continued grandly, "Got some new rules! I want my shoes shined every morning and my coffee hot with a danish on the side . . ."

Through the general store's window, Waffles, Mr.

Snuggles, and a bunch of other critters marveled at the chameleon's cool courage in the face of danger.

Rango stopped strutting. He suddenly became aware of the presence of . . . the HAWK!

He hastily concluded his speech, "Of course, there's no need for violence as long as we stick together, work as a team. So I want you all to come outside now and line up single file while I take a brief intermission."

The chameleon darted into the outhouse and slammed the door.

"What's he doing now?" Priscilla asked from the safety of the store.

"I—I think it's number two," Waffles guessed.

The chameleon cowered inside the smelly shed. Suddenly, the hawk's talons tore through the outhouse.

Hazel Moats seized the opportunity to rush into the street to reclaim his hat. His sudden movement made the hawk turn. So Hazel retreated, muttering, "Never mind." Better to lose a hat than his head!

Rango ran out of the collapsed remains of the outhouse, trailing toilet paper like a coward's flag at half-mast. The hungry hawk chased after him.

Inside the saloon, terrified townsfolk ran from one window to another to catch glimpses of the chameleon's progress.

Elbows the cat elbowed his way closer to the window to get a better view of the action.

Buford watched the lizard streaking down Main Street at top speed and remarked, "Well, look at him now."

From their limited point of view, it was hard for those inside the store to tell who was chasing whom. Was this amazingly brave (or IQ-challenged) stranger actually chasing the hawk?!

"Give him heck, Rango!" Elgin shouted.

Soon Rango found himself in the roadrunner stables. He scooted through the door, hoping the hawk had not seen him.

Startled roadrunners reared up on hind legs and stomped in their stalls. Bridles and saddles rattled on their hooks against the rough walls.

Rango spotted an ancient vending machine and scrambled inside. The chameleon slipped into a package of licorice. He had no time to wonder if his tasty disguise would work. The hawk suddenly slammed into the machine!

Rango shuddered. He did NOT want to be the hawk's next meal!

The hawk's attack forced a coin to fall into the coin slot. Something shifted inside the vending machine, and a piece of candy dropped down. It was the package of licorice in which Rango was hiding!

With lightning speed, the lizard shrugged out of the glossy paper. The hawk reached for its prize, but claimed only an empty wrapper.

Rango ran away from the stables down Main Street. Licorice was tied around his waist, dragging behind him like a bride's train. The clever hawk grabbed the trailing licorice.

With one tug, the bird of prey could pull Rango into its beak! But the little lizard grabbed one of the support beams holding up the town's empty water tower and clung on desperately.

The hawk tugged at the licorice. Rango took out his weapon and aimed at the candy string.

BANG! PING! PING! KA-POW!

Suddenly the cable supporting the water tower snapped in two. The tower tumbled over . . . and killed the hawk!

The stunned townspeople peeked out from their hiding places.

"Did you see that?" asked Mr. Furgus, the storekeeper. He never would have expected the little lizard could bring down the big hawk!

Buford the frog also had trouble believing what he had seen. He turned to the kooky, one-eared rabbit and asked, "What do you think, Doc?"

Doc was a long way from medical school. But he knew this much: "That hawk is dead!"

The townspeople looked at each other with growing excitement. Could it be? Dare they hope? Had Dirt at last found a true champion?

Waffles declared, "About time we had a hero 'round here."

"I think it's time he met the mayor," Buford suggested.

Spoons turned to the stunned chameleon. "You hear that, Rango? You're going to meet the mayor."

Elbows addressed the assembled group, "Let's hear it for Rango!"

WAAAAHOO!s and YEEE-HAAA!s echoed up and down the dusty street. Rango struggled to believe that

his dream had finally come true. He was a hero!

On a nearby rooftop, the owl mariachis strummed, plucked, and bowed their instruments as their leader, Señor Flan, commented on the latest turn of events.

"And so the stranger savored the adulations of his new friends . . . sinking deeper into the guacamole of his own deception."

Lupe, the violinist, wondered, "When is he going to die?"

Señor Flan assured, "Soon, compadre . . . soon."

# CHAPTER 5

# BELIEVE

**THE MAYOR** was busy when Rango arrived. He waited in the reception area with a foxy-looking fox named Angelique, the mayor's receptionist.

Rango idly picked up one of the mayor's golf clubs and took a swing. Suddenly, a loud, familiar voice came from the inner office.

"My land is not for sale!" Beans shouted.

Startled, Rango knocked a case of golf balls off the wall. The balls scattered across the fancy carpet. He hoped the pretty receptionist didn't think he was too much of a klutz.

Mr. Merrimack tried to calm the cowgirl. "Now Beans, he didn't mean to offend you!"

The office doors flew open and Beans stomped out. The banker followed.

Beans complained, "I came here to save my land, not sell it!"

The banker tripped over one of the scattered golf balls. His pudgy legs kicked out from under him. Undeterred, Mr. Merrimack stumbled after the departing cowgirl.

Angelique turned to Rango. "The mayor will see you now."

Rango found the old tortoise sitting in his wheelchair holding an eyedropper over an empty terrarium. The mayor carefully released a single drop of water from the glass tube as he explained, "Water . . . Mr. Rango . . . Water . . ."

Rango's eyes locked on the liquid. How he longed for a sip—and more!

"Without it, there's nothing but dust and decay. But with water, there's life," the mayor continued.

Tiny mites appeared and scurried toward the vital fluid.

"Look at them," the mayor told Rango. "So desperate to live, they will follow the water anywhere. That's the immutable law of the desert. Control the water, and you control everything."

The old tortoise glanced up at Rango, adding, "But I

don't need to tell you that, being a true man of the West as you are."

"Oh yeah," Rango agreed hastily. "The West is the best."

The mayor unlocked a cabinet and removed an elegant glass decanter. "This is from my private stock. Vintage rainwater."

Rango laughed politely. He felt much more thirsty than amused.

The mayor took out two glasses and tilted the fancy decanter, as if to pour. Rango's Adam's apple bowed to the mighty liquid. How he longed for water's soothing trickle!

"I guess power has its privileges," Rango remarked.

The mayor tilted the vessel tantalizingly toward the glass, and then stopped before it could pour. "You make a good point, son. But with privileges come responsibility."

Rango licked his lips. Seeing water so close yet not being able to drink it was torture!

The mayor rolled across the office. His rattling wheelchair stopped in front of a beautiful leather box. "Heck, I was mayor here before there was a Dirt! And I

may just be a sentimental old turtle, but I think there's a future for this town . . . and I hope you'll be part of it."

He raised his empty glass and toasted, "To Dirt!"

Rango lifted his dry glass toward his parched lips and politely pretended to drink.

The mayor and Rango moved to the office's balcony, a lofty perch above the whole town.

"You see all my friends and neighbors," the mayor began. "It's a hard life here. Very hard. You know how they make it through each and every day? They believe. They believe it's going to be better. They believe that the water will come. They believe against all odds and all evidence that tomorrow will be better than today."

He stared at Rango, looking deeply into both of the chameleon's oddly-shaped eyes. "People have to believe in something . . . and right now, they believe in you."

He opened the leather box on his lap and revealed a heap of shiny sheriff stars that gleamed like gems. The mayor removed one and set it on the top of the box.

"Pick it up, Mr. Rango," he urged, smiling broadly and revealing large teeth spaced out like tombstones. "Your destiny awaits."

As soon as Rango sauntered out of the mayor's office, Bad Bill emerged from the shadows.

"It's almost noon," the mayor stated. "Is everything ready?"

"Yeah," Bad Bill replied. "But he might be a problem."

The mayor grinned a greasy, gap-toothed smirk. "Mr. Rango is not a problem, William. He's a solution."

\* \* \*

At that moment, Rango felt like one of the legendary leads in his terrarium plays. But this was even better. It was real life! In the short time since the crash, could Rango really have become a hero and now a genuine, bonafide lawman with the silver star to prove it?

On Main Street, the big clock ticked closer to noon. Beans waited with Mr. Merrimack near her wagon outside the general store. It was Wednesday, and all the townsfolk were watching the clock.

Meanwhile, Beans and Mr. Merrimack pondered the mystery of the dry spell.

"It just doesn't make sense," said Beans. "The whole town is drying up, and the mayor is the only one who doesn't seem to be affected. Doesn't that make you just a

wee bit suspicious? And what about that water I saw out in the desert? 'Cause I've seen it with my own eyes."

Mr. Merrimack tried to soothe the troubled lizard. "Alright . . . alright. There's no need to incite anxiety. I'll inquire about the mayor. But if you really feel there's some conspiracy occurring, I suggest you take it up with the new sheriff."

Mr. Merrimack pointed to the store's front window. Behind it, Rango posed in front of a mirror in a slick suit. Mr. Black, a black widow spider wearing a formal black coat and top hat, moved swiftly around the new sheriff, tugging at a sleeve here and a hem there as he took various measurements with his tape measure.

Beans winced when she saw the chameleon admiring his reflection. This town needed help desperately—not a fashion show!

But many in Dirt were already treating Rango like a celebrity, including the mayor's pretty receptionist, Angelique, who stood near the mirror. Other customers whispered and stared. The little lizard who had once performed only for a dead bug, a headless doll, and a windup fish had come a long way!

Rango had never been fitted for a suit before. He

hadn't realized it would be such a prickly process. "Watch that needle there!" he said as the spider moved soundlessly from one side of the sheriff to the other.

Beans walked toward him, disgusted by the whole spectacle, especially the fawning presence of Angelique. As Rango tried on another hat, Beans interrupted, "Excuse me, Sheriff Rango, I want to talk to . . ."

Rango was glad to see the pretty lizard. "Hey, Beans! What do you think of the new duds? I got a ten-gallon hat marked down from fifteen."

"That's nice," Beans said without caring, eager to move on to more important subjects.

A young rat named Lucky tugged on Rango's back and held up his autograph book hopefully. "Excuse me, Mr. Rango, I was just thinking that I . . ."

The sheriff spun around and smiled. He'd always dreamed of signing autographs.

Beans grew more impatient. Would Rango be signing autographs when the town dried up and blew away?

"Sheriff, this isn't a social call," the cowgirl began. "I'd like to file . . . I need you to investigate . . ."

"You know, Beans, I bet you'd clean up real nice if you put a little effort into it," Rango commented. The

new sheriff did not pay any attention at all to what Miss Beans was trying to tell him.

The frustrated cowgirl continued, "Sheriff Rango, if that is your real name . . . I am trying to save my daddy's ranch, which is on the verge of an agricultural meltdown!"

Fury froze Beans in mid-rant.

Rango stared at the frozen lizard. Her face made him want to sing passionate Spanish riffs, but not when she was frozen!

The sound of hammering brought Beans out of her trance. The cowgirl continued talking as if nothing had happened, although on a completely different subject. Beans took a deep breath, and then remarked, "I did it again, didn't I?"

"Did what?" Rango asked with false innocence.

Beans sighed. She liked this strange, skinny chameleon. But sometimes Rango really got on her nerves. He seemed so sure of himself, but would Rango really help her town—or even survive the afternoon?

"Let me ask you something," said Beans as she pointed outside. "Did anybody here mention what happened to our last sheriff?"

Back on Main Street, Mr. Black was working hard in the sun, busily hammering nails into a new coffin.

Rango realized Mr. Black must be Dirt's undertaker—not its tailor. The chameleon struggled to swallow, but between fear and his intensely dry mouth, it was a slow and painful process.

Suddenly, the big clock began to toll, and everyone in the store dropped what they were doing and started moving slowly toward the door.

Puzzled, Rango followed the townsfolk, who seemed like they were sleepwalking or under hypnosis. Everyone held some kind of bottle, bucket, glass, or other container.

As they gathered together, Rango tried to find out what happened to the last sheriff, but the mesmerized mob ignored his questions.

"Um . . . excuse me . . . may I ask? The last sheriff? Pardon me . . . where is everybody going? What exactly happened to . . ."

No one answered Rango. They were too busy forming a long line. Then they started to dance to Hank Williams' legendary song "Cool Water." Rango had never seen anything like it.

The sheriff stepped into the line between a big, one-legged Native American fowl called Wounded Bird and little Priscilla.

"Well . . . this is a heck of a hoedown you got going," Rango began.

"Every Wednesday, just like clockwork," Priscilla replied.

Wounded Bird had something completely different to say. "Bird gone. Snake come."

"Snake?!" Rango asked in alarm.

"He means Rattlesnake Jake, Mr. Rango," Priscilla explained. "He never came to town 'cause he was scared of that hawk. But he might come now. Can I have your boots when you're dead?"

Rango shouted, "No!" Then he quickly boasted, "And I got no problem with this Rattlesnake Jake."

"That's just what Amos said!" Priscilla recalled and pointed to one of the many tombstones poking out of the dust in Dirt's cemetery.

The gray slab said "HERE LIES AMOS. BELOVED SHERIFF. TUESDAY–FRIDAY."

The chameleon read more tombstones, an alarming number of which marked the remains of previous

sheriffs. Despite his dry mouth, Rango gulped.

"You got any gold fillings?" Priscilla wondered.

Rango looked away from Priscilla's greedy little face to the crowd's destination: a giant faucet.

The mayor's wheelchair perched atop some scaffolding built to the same height as the faucet.

"My fellow Dirtonians," the mayor addressed the crowd. "I welcome you to our great day of deliverance. Hallelujah!"

"Hallelujah!" the thirsty townspeople shouted as one.

The mayor continued, "We have a newcomer amongst us today, my friends. A man I think needs little introduction to you, so bold has been his entry into our fair society . . . Mr. Rango, would you step forward?"

Excited by both the prospect of being honored and of quenching his thirst, Rango grabbed a tin cup and moved to the front of the line.

He could barely believe he was about to finally, finally, get a drink of water! The dehydrated chameleon stood right under the huge faucet, mouth twitching with anticipation.

The townspeople started to chant.

"The time has come, my friends," the mayor stoked

their excitement. "The time that was foretold!"

"Hallelujah!" the townspeople shouted in a single, ecstatic voice.

"The sacred time!" the mayor exclaimed with the perfect timing of a practiced politician or preacher. "It is the time of . . . HYDRATION!"

The townsfolk's chant built to an awe-inspiring crescendo as the spigot was turned. Every dry throat among them swallowed in delicious anticipation of the cool, clear water about to pour from that tall tap.

At last the spigot completed a full revolution. The faucet was open and . . .

. . . Nothing!

The crowd gasped in disbelief. Where was the cool, clear water? They held their breath and waited for that wonderful rush and flow, but . . .

GLOOP! One big glob of mud dropped from the spigot right down onto Rango. The slimy mass coated his head and dripped down onto his skinny shoulders.

SPLAT! Mud covered the chameleon until he looked like a chocolate-covered lizard.

The mayor tried to calm the crowd. "My friends, temper your frustrations. Times will be tough from now

on. Sacrifices will have to be made, but if I can help in any way, please know that my door is always open."

Beans interrupted the flow of the politician's platitudes. "Hold it! Now this whole thing stinks worse than a polecat's unwashed pajamas. First, the bank's run dry and now this here spigot . . ."

Beans' words spread panic like wind fanning the flames of a wildfire burning across dry prairie.

"Bank's run dry?" various citizens asked in alarm.

"What's she talking about?" Mr. Snuggles demanded. Every one of his quills stood on edge in sheer fear.

Bonnie Oats was still reeling from the discovery that her life savings didn't even pour out to a pint. She felt almost glad to hear that everyone else in Dirt was in the same situation.

Bonnie repeated, "She said there's no water in the bank!"

Everyone stared at Beans and then ran back to the bank. They ran without regard for safety, tripping and tumbling over each other like crazed cattle stampeding at a thunderclap.

At the bank, Mr. Merrimack and Parsons struggled to hold back the herd. Frantic customers called out

"Them's my liquid assets!" and "Close my rehydration account!"

"Hold on now!" Mr. Merrimack exclaimed, showing the crowd the almost empty bottle of water. "Hold on! This is all we have. We can't give it all out."

This alarming statement only made the mob even more hysterical.

Before the chaos could continue, Sheriff Rango declared, "We'll have none of that civil disobedience in my town, thank you."

He swaggered toward the bank teller's gate. By this point he performed Mr. Snuggles' walk even better than the porcupine himself.

Mr. Merrimack gushed in gratitude, "Thank goodness you're here, Sheriff. Things are getting out of hand."

The banker opened the gate to let Rango inside. The crowd pushed in behind him.

Rango strutted to the round, glass-fronted bank vault. "Ah . . . now let's take a gander at the source of the societal discontentment here," Rango began.

The sheriff looked at the giant jar. The slosh of water in it seemed barely enough to slake his own unbearable thirst, much less satisfy the entire town.

Rango gasped, "Mercy . . ."

Then he noticed the markings on the side of the bottle which indicated that the town had six days' worth of the precious fluid.

Rango addressed the crowd, "Alright, listen up. I've been thinking, and I believe I figured something out. You folks have a water problem."

Everyone grumbled. Why was the sheriff wasting time stating the obvious? The herd of thirsty townsfolk stared back at him bewildered. All they could think of was WATER, cool, clear water. Water was their currency; they must have water or die!

Rango sighed, "Now look here. We've got six days of water . . ."

With a quiet WHOOSH some air escaped from the bottle. The water line dropped below the five-day mark.

Rango tried not to let the audience perceive his panic. "We've got five days," he went on quickly. "As long as we've got water, we've got ourselves a town."

The mayor looked at Rango. An idea glowed behind the old tortoise's beady eyes.

"Sheriff Rango is right," the mayor stated. "So long as we have this water, we have some hope."

"And you can all take it from me, my one hundred percent full-time employment from this moment on will be to protect our precious natural resource," the lizard assured them with his best steely hero stare. Then he added, "No one's going to tango with the Rango."

# CHAPTER 6

# A POSSE AND A PROMISE

**THAT NIGHT,** Sheriff Rango strutted down Main Street wearing the nifty new duds stitched by the town's undertaker/tailor. He tipped his ten gallon hat to Melonee and her friend, Fresca, with a gallant, "Evening, ladies."

"Evening, Sheriff," both girls said at the same time.

The sheriff swaggered toward the saloon. Light music leaked through the gaps above and below its swinging double doors.

Suddenly, a burly critter tossed out a smaller customer named Gordy.

"Don't you come back!" warned the big critter.

Like all heroes, Rango hated to see bullying in any form. So he retrieved Gordy's hat, spun him around, and pushed him back into the saloon.

"Whoa! Hold on there, Gordy," Rango began. "Now

you get back in there and assert yourself. And I think you'll find the people of this here town to be surprisingly hospitable."

"Thank you, Sheriff," Gordy said.

But as soon as Gordy stepped foot in the place . . . SMASH! The bully threw Gordy right through the window.

Glass tinkled all around the sheriff's shiny boots as he murmured, "I stand corrected."

Rango looked from the shattered glass up the road. Something, or more accurately someone, popped up in the middle of Main Street.

The ground erupted, pushed up by two hillbilly prairie dogs. Ezekiel and his brother, Jedidiah, pushed their heads out of the fresh hole.

Jedidiah looked around in surprise. "This isn't the bank."

Ezekiel slapped his brother's head. "I told you, Jedidiah!"

The brothers had been too busy arguing to notice the sheriff's approach. Rango's deep, manly voice startled them.

The dogs panicked when they saw the sheriff's star

gleaming in the moonlight. The last thing they wanted to see was a lawman!

"Get your hands up where I can see 'em," Rango commanded,

Ezekiel and Jedidiah slowly raised their dirty hands.

Rango went on, completely misreading the situation. "Just as I suspected: prospectin' without the authorized equipment. Don't move a muscle."

He swaggered away, leaving the puzzled prairie dogs to consult with each other.

Jedidiah turned to his brother, "Prospectin'?"

Ezekiel shrugged.

Rango soon returned, weighed down with supplies. In his most official tone, he said, "Now, you got your shovel, pickaxe, Benadryl, loofah, assorted snacks, and puzzle books. And you're gonna need a permit."

From inside the tunnel, both gophers received a sound thrashing with a thick stick. Their old, blind Pappy whacked them impatiently. Why weren't they moving? Why weren't they proceeding with the robbery?

Pappy cussed, "Ezekiel! Jedidiah! What in the Sam Hill is going on up there?! I've had polyps removed smarter than the two of you!"

Ezekiel interrupted urgently, "Pappy! The sheriff is standing right here, helping us out!"

"Gonna give us a permit for prospecting," Jedidiah added, trusting that Pappy would play along with their amazing good luck.

"That's right, sir," Rango added politely. "Just doing my duty. The lonely constable on his rounds, keeping an eagle eye out for mayhem and malfeasance."

Pappy suppressed a wily grin. "Well, Sheriff, if we was to hit the motherload, being prospectors and such, where would we deposit said annuity?"

"Well, here in the town of Dirt we have the finest financial institution this side of the Missouri," Rango began. As he pointed toward the bank, the pompous sheriff concluded, "Protected morning, noon, and night by yours truly."

Rango handed Pappy the paper permitting him to dig for gold and silver in the dirt around Dirt. The chameleon gulped a piece of cactus fruit and then sighed contentedly. He was really starting to like this role.

Rango fell asleep that night feeling on top of the world. He could barely believe that he had so suddenly changed from caged chameleon to real live sheriff! To

the thirsty little lizard it seemed the stars shined a bit brighter that night.

But the next morning, Main Street woke to the bank teller's shout, "THE BANK'S BEEN ROBBED! THE BANK'S BEEN ROBBED! IT'S ALL GONE! THE WATER IS ALL GONE!"

Mr. Furgus stumbled out of the store, wondering aloud, "What's going on?"

"What's going on?" Mordecai asked his mother.

"What'd he say?" Mr. Snuggles' tall, skinny friend, Slim, asked.

"He said the bank's been robbed," the porcupine reported.

At that moment the law in Dirt still slumbered with cucumber slices cooling his celebrity eyelids. At Parsons' plaintive wail and the subsequent commotion, Rango bolted awake, confused and still half-lost in a nightmare.

On the roof above the sheriff's office, the owl mariachis sang of Rango's certain failure. For at that moment, the town was completely and most assuredly broke.

Rango quickly peeled the vegetables off his eyes and

swaggered to the bank. He pushed his way through the crowd to the vault.

Through the round glass door, Rango could plainly see that Parsons was right. The big bottle of reserve water was gone! Where it had rested, Rango saw a freshly-dug hole in the floor.

The sheriff recited every phrase he'd ever heard on a police show. "Alright, folks, stand back. This is a crime scene now. Clear the area, secure the perimeter, dust for prints, check for fibers, and scan for DNA."

Rango went on, "I want a urine sample from everyone, and get me a latte." Then he added, "And don't mix up the two."

Parsons found a piece of paper near the hole. He picked it up and read, "Prospecting Permit."

Rango snatched the paper, suddenly painfully aware of his incredibly stupid mistake. "I'll take that. Material evidence." He tucked the permit in his pocket, hoping no one would remember it.

"What are we gonna do now, Sheriff?!" someone wondered.

"We need that water!" Spoons exclaimed in a hoarse voice.

Just then the mayor's wheelchair smoothly glided up beside the sheriff, and the old tortoise announced, "Well, we all know what we have to do now."

"That's right. We all know what we have to do now!" Rango agreed automatically. Then he prompted the mayor. "And that would be . . . ?"

"Form a posse," the politician hissed quietly to the sheriff.

Rango didn't quite understand the tortoise's wheezy whisper. But he repeated it loudly anyway, "FORM A OPOSSUM!"

This absurd suggestion was met with stunned silence.

The mayor whispered more distinctly, "A posse."

This time Rango recited correctly, "Form a posse!"

The townsfolk quickly assembled on Main Street near the big clock tower.

"What do we do now, Sheriff?" asked Mr. Furgus.

Rango's eyes narrowed with dramatic intensity as he answered the storekeeper, "Now, WE RIDE!"

Just about every able-bodied man in town, plus Beans, joined Sheriff Rango's posse. The whole town felt swept up in an exciting adventure.

The posse raced out of town, whipping their road runners over the dusty trail. The mariachi owls played rousing rhythms inspired by the beat of the running birds' feet.

After a while, stinky old Spoons caught up to Rango to ask, "Where are we goin'?"

The sheriff blinked one eye, and then the other. In the thrill of riding, Rango had forgotten to choose a destination. He had no clue where they were headed!

The posse turned around and rode back to Main Street. Soon Rango pinned a homemade deputy star on the one-legged creature known as Wounded Bird who had a reputation of always knowing where he was going and the ability to track anything.

Rango told Wounded Bird, "Now as my deputy you'll be in charge of all trackin' and findin' of villains. So which way do you think they went?"

Wounded Bird pointed to the big prairie dog hole left in the middle of Main Street.

Rango nodded, pleased with his deputy's answer. "Oh, you're good."

As each member of the posse jumped down into the hole, the sheriff offered encouragement.

"Now I'm depending on you, Spoons," he told the old mouse.

Rango greeted the one-eared rabbit, "Always good to have a medical man along, Doc."

The rabbit joined Spoons down the hole.

To Buford, the frog, Rango said, "Reptiles gotta stick together, right, my brother?"

The frog sulked, "I'm an amphibian."

"There's no shame in that," Rango told him heartily.

Buford leaped down the hole, revealing the next volunteer in the long line: a uniform-clad bird that looked as bad as Roadkill! But despite an arrow poking out of one of his eyes, Sergeant Turley seemed eager to serve.

Rango exclaimed, "Oh! You sure you're fit for duty there, soldier?"

The sergeant didn't know what Rango was talking about. "What?" he demanded.

Rango wasn't sure where to begin. "Well, you got a little something in your eye there."

Turley pointed to the eye without the arrow. "Oh that? That there is conjunctivitis, sir. It's, uh, hereditary."

Rango nodded and blustered, "Oh, well, glad to hear it's not contagious."

When it came to Beans' turn, Rango shook his head. "Now just wait one cotton-pickin' minute. A posse is no place for a . . ."

Beans didn't wait for permission. She just jumped down the hole, revealing the final volunteer: Priscilla.

Rango wasn't about to let the little girl risk her life by chasing bad guys. That was for brave heroes like him.

But Priscilla worried that the mission wouldn't succeed without her. "Sheriff, you are gonna bring that water back, aren't you?"

Rango promised, "Count on it, little sister." Then he dropped down into the tunnel.

Soon the posse was lost in a maze of tunnels beneath Dirt.

"Which way do we go, Sheriff?" Spoons asked.

"There are tunnels everywhere," Doc observed. "Just how did them fellers find the bank anyway?"

"Gentlemen, if we could just stay on task here," the sheriff said and quickly steered the conversation away from his error.

It was an honest mistake. Rango thought he was helping prospectors obey the law—not giving robbers directions to the bank!

Ambrose found an old, familiar-looking plumbing part. "Sheriff, over here!" he called excitedly.

"Would you look at that!" Buford exclaimed, recognizing the pipe.

"I remember when it used to flow every Wednesday," Mr. Furgus recalled.

Elgin scratched his head. "There must be a reason she quit on us."

Beans took a practical approach, "Well, whatever the reason, something is controlling this here water."

"What do you think, Sheriff?" Waffles wondered.

Rango spoke in a deep, serious tone using the biggest words he knew, "Clearly the robbers came from this direction. I say we track this pipe back to its hydraulic origin and apprehend the culprits behind this aquatic conundrum."

Buford nudged Turley, "What'd he say?"

Turley tilted his head till the arrow pointed at the pipe. "I think he said follow the pipe."

So the posse followed the pipe along several tunnels.

"Sure is humid down here," Spoons observed, wiping the moisture off his filthy beard.

Other members of the posse shared their complaints as well. But they kept walking through the maze of moist tunnels.

After a while, the group arrived in a large cavern. The chameleon shuddered when he saw what lay ahead: a narrow path on top of a crumbling stone bridge with no walls or handrails to protect them from falling off either side!

"Whatever you do, don't look down," Rango warned, before immediately looking down into the bottomless depths below. The dizzying distance nearly made Rango lose his footing. But he looked away just in time to recover with a loud "Whoa!"

"What is this place?" Waffles wondered aloud, even more jittery than usual.

Beans answered, "It's an aquifer."

"Ahhh . . ." Waffles said, adding, "What's an aquifer?"

"Well, it's for aqua," Buford reasoned.

"Well, it's empty now," Waffles concluded.

As the posse made its way across the top of the abandoned aquifer, a giant subterranean creature opened its eye. To this giant, the small town animal posse must have seemed like insignificant insects.

Everyone started breathing again when the creature closed its humongous eye and let the posse pass. But their troubles were far from over. The tunnel they had been following abruptly ended, and the group found themselves in front of a solid cave wall.

"It's the end of the line," Mr. Furgus declared.

"It doesn't go further," Spoons confirmed, touching the solid wall of dirt with his filthy paw.

"Trail cold," Wounded Bird agreed.

But Turley argued. "Well, now, that there's a pipe. It's got to be connected to somethin'."

"Yeah, well . . ." Elgin began. His slow vocabulary needed time to catch up to his swift temper.

Buford couldn't believe these folks were wasting their time arguing. He interrupted, "You just don't get it, do ya? Someone or somethin' is messing with our hydration and that pipe's got something to do with it."

Elgin was confused. "Now, I thought we were following bank robbers!"

"We are experiencing a paradigm shift," answered Turley.

Everyone looked at each other blankly. No one knew what Turley meant.

"I'm going to shift the features on your face if you don't pipe down," threatened Elgin. He didn't need to understand what someone said to start a fight with them.

The argument between Elgin and Turley touched off others among the tired posse. Fear took its toll, causing the crew to erupt into chaos.

Voices grew louder and angrier. Tempers flared hotter than the flaming torches the volunteers carried. Fists shot up in the air as the posse violently debated such vital questions as: Where should they go? What should they do now? And whose fault was it that they'd reached this dead end?

For a moment the cavern was as quiet as a library after closing hours. Then Rango suddenly cried, "Whoa! I got it! Snuff out the torches."

The posse was puzzled. But they trusted Rango. So they did as their sheriff asked, plunging the cavern into complete darkness.

Everyone blinked. At first they saw nothing but pitch blackness. But soon they noticed a sliver of light shining down from above them.

"Start climbin'," Waffles suggested.

As the posse's eyes adjusted to the dim light, the outlines of thick, twisted roots became as clear as day. They led up from the ground to the cavern's ceiling. The entire posse followed the nervous toad's suggestion and climbed toward the light.

Rango felt proud that he was able to get them out of this mess. Finally, he had done something right. He couldn't help but brag to the pretty cowgirl. "Not bad, huh, Beans?"

Beans wished the oddly appealing chameleon would stop being so vain. She teased, "You keep thinking like that and your hat's going to catch fire."

Rango took his ten-gallon bargain off of his torch and put it back on his head so Beans would get the full sheriff-y effect. It suddenly burst into flames!

"WHOA! HOT! HOT. BURN. WHOA. OW!" the sheriff shouted as he struggled to smother the fire.

The climbing posse ignored his clumsy calamity, but that didn't stop Rango from trying to take charge as usual.

"I got it! I'm okay," he said when he had finally extinguished the last of the sparks.

# CHAPTER 7

## STARLIT LEGENDS

**EAGER TO GET OUT** from underground at last, the posse kept climbing higher and higher. At the top, they pushed through the small opening and climbed out. Rango and others emerged onto the bright, hot sand, blinking like moles.

Several dark shapes littered the sand around them. They were dead cacti.

Beans tenderly patted the wrinkled green vegetation between its sharp spikes. "Poor things. All they wanted was a little water."

Mr. Furgus swallowed drily. "A cactus dying of thirst? That doesn't bode well for us."

Waffles saw a metal canteen lying on the ground and reached for it excitedly. "Hey, hey! Look what I found!"

Thirsty for what could be liquid contents, Elgin

grabbed for the canteen and exclaimed, "Hey, I saw that first!"

Several others joined in the struggle.

"He found some water!" Turley shouted, adding to the chaos.

"That's mine!" Waffles declared.

"Hold on! Give me that!" Elgin objected, grunting with effort to wrestle it out of the toad's grasp.

But Waffles wouldn't let go, and the two critters played tug of war with the canteen until it opened and fell, dumping nothing but hot air onto the already sizzling sand.

The thirsty posse was utterly disappointed. Elgin kicked the sand in frustration.

Rango was just about to figure out a plan when Ambrose called from the next dune. He was standing in front of a dark heap on the pale sand—and it sure as shootin' wasn't a cactus.

"Sheriff, you're gonna wanna see this!" he called out.

Rango and the rest of the posse quickly gathered by Ambrose.

Beans spoke first, "It's Mr. Merrimack from the bank . . ."

"What's he doing here?" Ambrose asked.

"Everybody stand back," Rango instructed.

Doc stepped forward, seeing that the situation called for a professional medical opinion. "Alright, let me see."

"Looks like them varmints got him in the back," Spoons concluded for no reason at all.

Doc shook his head. "No, this man was drowned!"

Buford wondered if Doc might have a screw loose rattling around with all that medical know-how. Doc's conclusion didn't seem possible. Buford asked skeptically, "Drowned . . . ?"

"In the middle of the desert?" Waffles added.

Then Elgin noticed red-mud boot prints near the body. "Well, now, whose boot prints are those?" he asked.

Rango crouched down to examine the prints more closely. He touched the reddish soil near one of the impressions and remarked, "That's interesting. The ground's still wet."

Beans sighed. She would miss Mr. Merrimack—even if he had denied her credit.

The posse agreed they should pay tribute to the town banker. It was the right thing to do.

"Sheriff, will you say a few words?" Spoons asked.

Never one to pass up a chance to hear his own voice, Rango quickly agreed and rattled off what he hoped would serve for a funeral.

"Dearly beloved, we are gathered here today to honor this man, Mr. Merrimack. You have the right to remain silent. Speak now or forever hold your peace. Amen."

"Amen," the posse echoed, satisfied that "a few words" had been spoken, even if they made no particular sense.

While everyone else was paying their respects, Wounded Bird stood alone on the hillside. He was pulling out some of his feathers and tossing them in the air.

In due course, the posse climbed the hill and joined him.

"Shh. Pick up trail," Wounded Bird began. He examined the ground, and then pronounced, "Three men, heading west. One blind; one riding sidesaddle."

Waffles would have sweated if he hadn't been so close to dying of thirst. The toad worried even at the best of times, and Wounded Bird's proclamation sounded like danger was headed their way. He fretted, "What exactly are we gonna do now?"

Rango knew it was time to get moving. He declared in his most inspiring voice, "Now, WE RIDE!"

The posse rode all that day, past towering mesas, through narrow canyons, and across smoldering sands. At intervals, the riders would stop just long enough to rest their roadrunners and for Wounded Bird to examine the trail.

That night, they made camp under the vast western sky and toasted marshmallows around a blazing fire.

The sticky treat made Waffles feel nostalgic. "Marshmallows remind me of going camping with my daddy. I could eat them all night long. Of course, he did make me cough them back up again for breakfast."

Buford's quick tongue suddenly flicked out of his mouth to snatch Waffles' flaming marshmallow. The frog belched, and then remarked, "This one time I coughed up an entire Dalmatian."

Nobody knew how to respond. In the awkward silence that followed, Spoons asked, "Mr. Rango, can you tell us about the Spirit of the West?"

"Oh, yeah, tell us about that!" Doc exclaimed, eager to hear about anything but the reappearance of digested food.

"Is it true what they say?" Waffles prompted.

Rango stared into the dancing flames and sighed dramatically. Acting wasn't just speaking; it existed in the pauses and movement as well.

The sheriff lifted a glowing stick from the fire and drew in the night sky as he spoke. "The eternally unattainable ideal . . . They say he rides in an alabaster carriage with golden guardians to protect him. But he only appears to those who have undertaken an epic quest and have made it to the other side."

"The other side of what?" Turley asked.

"It's a metaphor," Rango answered, recalling Roadkill's annoyingly mystical words.

For a moment, the only sounds came from the crackling fire and the distant yelps of hungry coyotes. Then the topic of conversation changed to Rattlesnake Jake.

Rango quickly bluffed. "Oh, yeah, Jake. You mean my brother."

Turley was amazed that the small sheriff could be related to such terrifying kin. "Rattlesnake Jake is your brother?"

"That's what I said," Rango replied.

Buford scratched his head. The frog didn't know much more than how to pour cactus juice, but even he knew that brothers had to be the same species.

"Did he ever bite you?" Mr. Furgus asked.

"Sure enough did," Rango answered. He lifted up his shirt to display a small, round scar. The sheriff urged, "Look at that baby. Go ahead. You can touch it."

Doc piped in, unsure of what Rango was talking about. "That's interesting," he said. "That there is a belly button."

Rango paid the comment no heed and continued as if Doc hadn't uttered a single word. "Luckily I'm immune to his venom. I put some in my coffee just to give it a little tang."

"Is it true he's only scared of them hawks?" Waffles wondered. Then he shuddered just thinking about Jake and the hawk.

"That's what we call his natural predator," Rango stated.

Several coyotes howled, sounding closer to the campfire than before. Most of the posse members shivered with fear.

Mr. Snuggles moved a little closer to the fire. "All this

talk is putting my quills on edge."

"I'm not going to sleep tonight," Buford declared.

"Ah, don't you worry about a thing," Rango told his team. "Come tomorrow we'll locate that water and return to a hero's welcome."

Rango's speech was heartwarming and encouraging, but Spoons didn't want to take any chances. He stood up and announced, "Friends, before we bunk down, I'd like to join hands for a moment and say a few words to the Spirit of the West."

The rest of the posse murmured in agreement. They all stood and joined hands.

"Tonight I want to thank you for bringing Sheriff Rango into our lives," said Spoons.

Rango looked at all the sincere, faithful faces gathered around the fire. These folks really trusted him. He hoped they would never find out the truth that he was as phony as his name.

Spoons went on, "It's a hard life we got. Sometimes I don't know how we're going to make it. But somehow Sheriff Rango makes me think we will . . ."

Rango's eyes focused on the pretty lizard. Beans looked back at him with an expression Rango couldn't

read. Did she believe in him? Did she want to believe?

Spoons concluded, "We needed a brave man, and you sent us one. It's nice to have someone to believe in again. Thank you, Spirit of the West."

Soon a variety of snores surrounded the campfire. But the sheriff couldn't sleep, especially when he saw Beans standing alone on the crest of a hill.

The pretty lizard stood so still he thought she might be frozen again. Rango went to check on her. If Beans stayed out in the desert all night she might actually freeze.

Even up close, Rango couldn't be sure if she was stargazing or catatonic. He waved his hand in front of her face, and Beans turned to him. She had just been quietly enjoying the view.

Rango apologized, "Oh . . . I was just checking to see if you were okay. It's a little cold tonight." He gallantly arranged his blanket around her.

"Thank you," Beans said. When he wasn't bragging, Beans really liked Rango.

The chameleon stared out at the desert dotted with cacti that cast eerie shadows in the starlight. "Do you ever feel like those things are looking at you?"

Beans followed the sheriff's gaze. "Those are 'Spanish Daggers,' but around here we just call them 'Walking Cacti.'"

"Walking?" Rango asked.

Beans explained, "There's an old legend that they actually walk across the desert to find water." She paused a moment before saying, "When I was little I'd stay up late trying to catch them moving. I thought if I could follow them, they would lead me to someplace wonderful, someplace with enough water for everyone. Night after night I watched them, but I never saw them move."

"But you're still watching," Rango observed.

"Who doesn't want to find someplace wonderful?" Beans wondered wistfully. She gazed out over the valley in the distance. She wanted to believe in wonderful places—and a certain flashy hero.

As if sensing her need for reassurance, Rango said earnestly, "We'll find the water, Beans. I promise you."

Beans heard something new in the sheriff's voice. She looked up at the chameleon's face. Rango was serious!

Beans held his gaze until another coyote called. The forlorn howl seemed to echo through the pretty lizard's soul.

Despite the blanket, Beans shivered. "That's such a lonely sound. Do you ever get lonely?"

"Sure, sometimes," Rango said, thinking back on Mr. Timms, Dr. Marx, and the headless, one-armed doll. How could he admit that he had been lonely for all of his lizard life?

Beans shook her head. "I can't imagine it. You're such a charmer and everyone likes you so much." She sighed. "I never made friends easily. We were pretty isolated out there on the ranch. It was sort of like being sealed up in a little box. We didn't really see a lot of folks."

Rango wanted to blurt out, "I know exactly what you mean!" But Beans would probably hate him if she realized that Rango had been lying to her from the moment they met. So instead, he fibbed quietly, "I wouldn't know what that's like."

Beans finally summoned the courage to speak her mind. She looked away from the handsome sheriff shyly and asked, "Is there someone special in your life, Rango?"

The chameleon thought of all the love scenes he and the broken doll had played. Then he began, "Oh, well, there used to be, but she couldn't keep her head.

Besides, my life's too dangerous for that kind of thing. It's an awful solitary existence out there on the prairie, riding the ranges and such . . ."

His voice trailed off into silence. When Beans didn't respond, he turned to see her reaction. The cowgirl's pretty face was as still as the cacti. Was she frozen? Rango waved his hand in front of Beans's eyes.

"Beans? Uh, Beans?"

He waited for a reply, but the pretty lizard didn't even blink. So Rango gently leaned over and kissed her cheek. Then he sighed and walked back to camp.

As soon as Rango's back was turned, Beans smiled. She wasn't frozen at all.

# CHAPTER 8

# A TOUGH AUDIENCE

**THE NEXT DAY,** the posse hit the road again. The trail led toward a canyon. From a distance, the sides of the canyon didn't appear remarkable. But when Rango gazed through his spyglass, he saw that the canyon cliffs were carved with hundreds of holes that dotted the stone like the many windows of a skyscraper. They had happened upon a prairie dog town.

The sheriff stared, fascinated by the strange town. As far as he could tell, it looked completely deserted except for two critters that looked awfully familiar. They were two of the three prairie dogs that had broken into the bank vault!

Rango took a deep breath and tried to summon his inner hero as he watched the prairie dogs argue. Rango knew he was going to have to make his very first official

arrest—and he couldn't wait for his big moment. The chameleon lowered his spyglass and turned to Beans and Wounded Bird.

"Dysfunctional family. Need intervention," Wounded Bird stated. As usual, he was a bird of few words.

Beans saw a plume of dust moving across the desert. She asked, "What's that comin'?"

Rango raised the spyglass again. Through it he recognized Ezekiel, the third guilty prairie dog. Ezekiel's wagon was hauling the bank's water bottle under a tarp!

Rango gasped, "It's the water!"

By then, the rest of the posse had gathered around. Hope fluttered all around them like a beautiful butterfly. Perhaps Dirt would survive after all!

Rango knew the prairie dogs would not give up their liquid gold or their freedom without a fight, but that was not going to stop him from doing his job. He announced, "I have a plan, and each and every one of you has a part to play."

"What do I do?" Spoons asked excitedly.

Rango answered, "Spoons, you've got the most important job of all. You're going to stay up here on the ridge. If anything goes wrong, you give us the signal."

Before long, Rango told everyone else what they were supposed to do, too. While the posse prepared, Rango warmed up his voice. Tonight was going to be the performance of a lifetime.

"Mmma! Mmmaaaaa!" he hummed, just like he used to in his terrarium.

Now that all the parts were cast, it was time to put together some costumes. Rango asked the pretty cowgirl, "Hey, Beans, what size dress are you wearin'?"

★ ★ ★

In Dogtown, all the critters were celebrating Ezekiel's arrival—and the wagon with its precious cargo.

Jedidiah exclaimed, "Look! He got it! Pappy, he found the water!"

"Hallelujah!" Pappy exalted. "You did it, son!"

"Well, actually . . ." Ezekiel began sheepishly. Knowing he had a big problem, he tried to explain his side of the story. "Now, Pappy, about that water. There's somethin' I gots to tell ya."

Blind Pappy barely heard his son and ordered, "Shh! Hush up now. There's someone coming!"

The prairie dog's keen senses had alerted him to the presence of Rango and the posse. Of course, they

84

no longer looked like a posse. Rango was now wearing Beans' dress, and the others had donned makeshift Renaissance garb.

Instead of speaking in his fake Western drawl, the chameleon now cooed like a dramatic grande dame, "Whoa-oh! Ha-ha. Good sirs! Gracious good afternoon to thee . . . and thee . . . and thee! May I present Madame Lupone's Terpsichorean Troupe of Traveling Thespians!"

Pappy did not understand all of the stranger's long words. "Wha—what's that?"

"I think they're thespians," Ezekiel repeated.

"Thespians?" Pappy exclaimed. "That's illegal in seven states."

Just like the good ol' days in his terrarium, Rango held up two palm fronds as curtains while he narrated intently, "The stage is set. The princess prepares to meet her destiny."

This time Beans portrayed the distressed princess. Rango thought she looked beautiful!

Playing her part to a T, the cowgirl said sadly, "I yearn for love."

Rango went on without missing a beat, "Meanwhile, the lone sentry stands watch at the castle gate!"

For several seconds nothing happened. The cue just hung there in the silence. Then Rango repeated the line in a louder voice, with both eyes focused firmly on Elgin, "I SAID, 'STANDS WATCH AT THE CASTLE GATE!'"

Suddenly recognizing that it was his turn, Elgin recited, "Hark! Who goes there?"

In the audience, Pappy sighed. "This plot's highly predictable."

But Ezekiel was entranced, swept up by the theater's imaginative spell. He hissed, "Quiet! This is my favorite part."

Rango continued, "Arriving to great fanfare was her aged father."

Right on cue, the mariachi trumpets played. And then Sergeant Turley appeared, dressed as the king. The soldier was not accustomed to performing. He struggled with the unfamiliar words. "Um . . . Prithee unhand my fair daughter, and reach for the . . ."

Turley hesitated, unable to recall what he was supposed to say next. But Ezekiel knew exactly how to finish the line. He shouted, "Reach for the sky!"

As if in defiant response, the posse members surrounded the unsuspecting, dim-witted prairie dogs.

"We got you surrounded. So you and your entire family need to get your hands up where we can see 'em," Rango stated triumphantly.

Pappy chuckled. "My entire family?"

The puzzled posse suddenly heard a low rumble that seemed to come from everywhere at once. Hundreds of rodents poured out of holes in the cliff. They readied weapons ranging from pitchforks to rocket launchers.

The bucktoothed creatures chanted, "Grits 'n' spit 'n' collard greens . . . waffle chitlins, monkey brains . . . refried bones 'n' booger blood . . . pickled eggs 'n' flaps of mud."

The posse looked around. Every wall crawled with rodents eager to feud!

Rango had never seen so many pairs of eyes in one place before. After performing for no one but his own reflection for so many years, it was a truly awesome sight. "A full house," he cheered.

But of course, this audience was not interested in the play. They wanted to square off against Rango's posse!

"Looks like we got ourselves a good old-fashioned standoff," Pappy declared.

From a distant dune, Spoons shrieked like a crow, "Caw-caw-caw! Caw-caw . . . Caw . . ."

The smelly old mouse flapped his arms like crazy and literally raised a stink.

"What's that supposed to be?" Ezekiel wondered.

Elgin replied, "That's the signal."

"That's the signal!" Waffles exclaimed. "Something must be wrong."

Spoons waved two flags over his head and then ran over to the campfire and started to send smoke signals.

Rango's plan hadn't gone much further than to dress like actors, capture the dogs, and then ride back to Dirt in triumph. So far he had only succeeded in dressing like actors. He was fresh out of ideas on how to make the other two parts of his plan come to fruition.

"So . . . somethin' supposed to happen?" Pappy wondered.

"I'm open to suggestions," Rango said.

Before anyone could offer up a thought, Spoons collapsed from exhaustion. He raised his pistol and fired into the air. BANG!

The sound scared the javelina that was hitched to Ezekiel's wagon. It panicked and took off at top speed,

carting the water bottle away from the prairie dogs.

"RUN!" Rango shouted. He could not let the water get away! The sheriff and the posse raced toward the retreating vehicle.

"Get on the wagon!" Beans cried.

"Come on, everybody!" the sheriff shouted. "Get on the wagon! Hold on!"

Pappy stood back with his sons, unconcerned by the posse's hasty departure. He asked, "Should we have ourselves some sport, chill'ens?"

Jedidiah grinned. "I like it when they run."

Ezekiel, Jedidiah, and all their numerous relations pulled on aviator goggles. Excitement spread through the horde faster than a fever through a kindergarten.

"Maybelle, give the holler," Pappy instructed a rodent with pigtails and one platform boot.

Maybelle lifted her bare foot and let out a screeching cry that sounded like a yodel mixed with a fire engine siren.

At this amazing hog holler, every bucktoothed head simultaneously dropped out of sight. Soon, the entire town was deserted.

Rango and the others had a significant head start on

their foes. The posse clung desperately to the wagon as it careened through the narrow slot canyons surrounding Dogtown.

Waffles looked over his shoulder at the shrinking cliff. "Looks like we made it!"

Even with danger lurking around every corner, Rango could think of nothing but the show.

Suddenly a swarm emerged and streaked across the desert sky. The black cloud curled ominously from the cliff dwellings. As it neared, the posse discovered the cloud was alive—with bats! Riding cowboy-style atop each bat were prairie dogs. They hooted and hollered with wild abandon!

"We got bats on our tail!" Waffles reported.

Rango handed the reins to Beans. "Oh, here. You drive."

Beans snapped the reins, struggling to control the speeding wagon as the big water bottle lurched from side to side in the back.

The bats swooped in formation to attack. The prairie dogs cheered as they fired down on the posse. RAT-TAT-TAT-TAT! RAT-TAT-TAT-TAT!

"Yee-haw!" the rodents rejoiced.

Pappy called out, "Jedidiah! It's time for the Alabama squeeze box!"

"Okay, Pa!" Jedidiah eagerly agreed.

The bats dove in closer to the wagon.

"I'm sensing hostility," Waffles reported with growing alarm. The toad's lumpy skin twitched.

Two bats swooped down on each side of the wagon, and both riders drew their weapons on Rango and Beans!

"Hello," said one.

"Goodbye," said the other.

Rango pulled the brake just as both rodents fired—on each other! They smacked into the canyon walls.

Another rodent slammed into the back of the wagon, causing Rango to bounce out of his seat and onto the javelina. The sheriff struggled to stay above the large pig-like animal hauling the wagon—and not under her trampling feet!

"Lasso that swine!" Pappy commanded.

A rodent obediently and expertly slung a coiled rope over the sheriff's skinny shoulders. The rope pulled Rango off the javelina and into the air!

"WHOOOA!" Rango exclaimed.

Two rodent kids used their slingshot to send dynamite sticks flying out toward the wagon.

Ambrose saw the explosives and wisely advised, "I suggest we take evasive action."

"What happened to the sheriff?" asked Elgin.

"He had a previous engagement," Beans fibbed. She did not want the others to give up hope.

Amid the chaos and squeaking bats, Pappy commanded his squadron. "Boseefus, give 'em some gumbo now!"

Rodents dropped down on ropes to invade the retreating wagon.

"What was that?" Beans wondered at the THUD she heard at the back of the wagon. "Go check it out!" she told Waffles.

The toad peeked over the top of the wagon and saw one of the prairie dogs approaching holding two knives. Waffles was too scared to speak.

"What is it?" asked Beans, trying to keep her eyes on the path ahead. "Is there a problem?"

"Uh . . . you could call it that," Waffles managed to croak out.

Flying through the air without the greatest of ease,

92

Rango was just as frightened as Waffles. The chameleon's fragile nervous system was in overload. Everywhere he looked Rango saw rodents, rodents, and more rodents, shouting, speeding, and hooting!

The sheriff had never been in a real battle before. This unstructured mayhem was nothing like the carefully choreographed scenes of his terrarium triumphs.

Two gunners circled around to ambush the helpless sheriff, forcing Rango out of his terrified trance. The clumsy chameleon panicked. The next thing he knew, the two bats had collided and Rango had landed on a third bat! As he tried to control the veering flyer, he accidentally dropped one of the sticks of dynamite strapped to the creature's saddle.

BOOM! A rock pillar fell directly in front of the posse's wagon. Unable to stop, Beans managed to maneuver the vehicle just under the pillar, knocking off the knife-wielding rodent riding in the back!

Rango's clumsiness had managed to defeat the hawk. Would his luck hold out?

True to form, the answer turned out to be no. The bat had had enough and bucked Rango off his back. Rango spiraled down, free falling with Bean's dress billowing

through the air. The sheriff landed right on top of Spoons' speeding roadrunner. His skirt completely covered the old mouse.

Spoons peeked out from beneath Beans' calico dress and remarked, "Surprisingly, that wasn't altogether unpleasant."

Rango and Spoons rode on and caught up to the wagon. Beans bravely battled a rodent and swatted it off the wagon.

"Get your hands off me!" she shouted, kicking off another while still holding onto the bouncing reins.

Rango admired the girl's courage, but he knew heroes didn't let damsels defend themselves alone. So he leaned over, grabbed hold of the wagon, and swung into the front seat.

SMACK! Unfortunately, Beans was so used to hitting anything that came near her that she whacked Rango right in the face.

The pair barely had time to react when—BAM!—the wagon wheels hit a large rock, sending the posse careening out of control!

"Jump!" Rango and Beans shouted in unison and leapt to safety.

The wagon crashed and the valuable water bottle rolled off into the desert. Posse and rodents all rushed to see if the precious liquid would survive the wreck.

Many pairs of eyes took in the terrible truth at once. The water bottle was not only broken . . . it was EMPTY!

The posse studied the broken jug. There wasn't a single drop of water, but the critters did find something of interest: Mr. Merrimack's spectacles.

Waffles had a hard time believing that all of Dirt's water was truly gone. "It's impossible."

Beans tried to make sense of it as well. "It can't be empty," she said hopefully.

A thirsty rodent kid mourned, "There's no water . . ."

Pappy exclaimed, "No water?! What the heck have we been fightin' for?"

Rango replied with indignation, "Sir, you have defiled and desecrated the very sustenance of our livelihood."

Jedidiah suddenly recognized Rango from his fancy way of speaking. "I think that there fella in the pretty dress is the sheriff."

"The same fella who gave us our prospecting permit?" Pappy asked.

"What?" Beans queried, completely confused.

Rango hoped to steer the subject away from his embarrassing mistake. He quickly declared, "Irrelevant! Obfuscation!"

Then he told Pappy in his most authoritative tone, "You and your kin are under arrest for the bank robbery—and the murder of our beloved financial advisor, Johannes Merrimack the third, also known as Fluffy Joe."

Ezekiel objected, "Sheriff, we didn't kill anybody. We tunneled into that vault—but there was nothin' in it."

Jedidiah added, "Somebody robbed the bank before we robbed it!"

Beans looked from the empty bottle to the prairie dogs dubiously. She demanded, "So where did you get this here jug?"

Ezekiel sighed. "That's what I've been trying to tell Pappy. I found it in the desert."

"Then why in tarnation did you bring it here?!" Pappy exclaimed with great irritation and whacked his son over the head with his walking stick.

Rango tried to figure out what was going on. "Hold

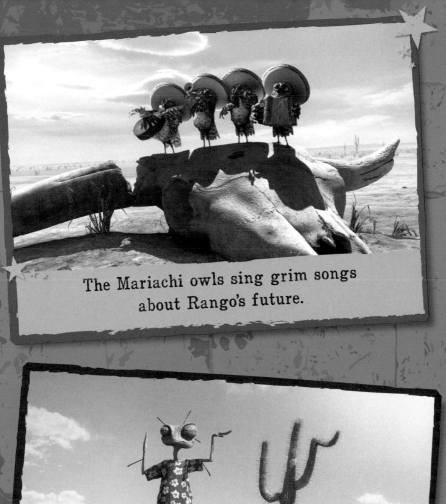

The Mariachi owls sing grim songs about Rango's future.

Rango tries to blend in with his surroundings to avoid danger.

The hawk sneaks up behind an unsuspecting Rango.

Priscilla is skeptical of Rango when he arrives in Dirt.

Bad Bill and his gang challenge
Rango to a showdown!

Pappy and the rodents ride bats to
chase Rango and his posse.

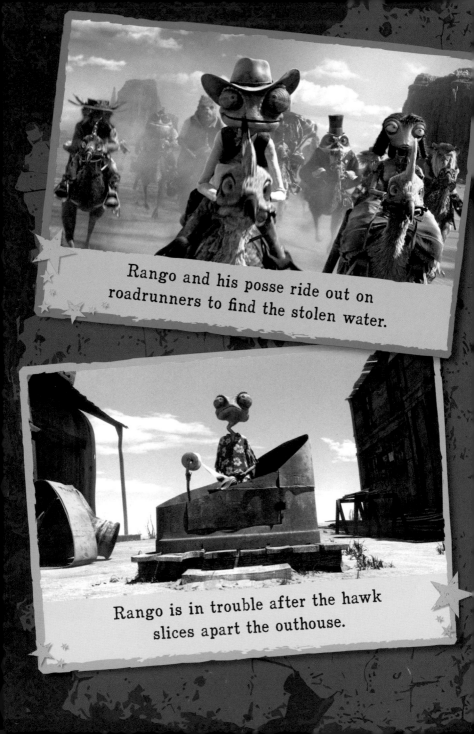

Rango and his posse ride out on roadrunners to find the stolen water.

Rango is in trouble after the hawk slices apart the outhouse.

The hawk's talons are sharp enough
to cut through metal!

In the saloon, Rango tells tall tales
about his past.

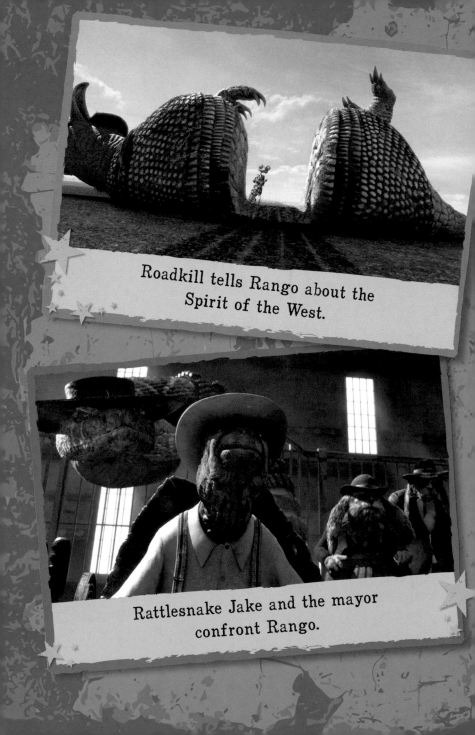

Roadkill tells Rango about the
Spirit of the West.

Rattlesnake Jake and the mayor
confront Rango.

# ★ BEHIND THE SCENES ★

The amazing art and life-like animation for *Rango* was not made overnight. It took artists and illustrators months to perfect every last detail of the characters. Before making it to the big screen, the talented team at Industrial Light and Magic created hundreds of character and set sketches, sculptures, and paintings for inspiration and research. Their animation experts then took that hand-drawn artwork and used it as a basis for the final CGI (computer-generated imagery) animation you see in theaters. Here is some "behind-the-scenes" art that shows how *Rango* came to life.

Original sketches of Rango

Heroic painting of Rango

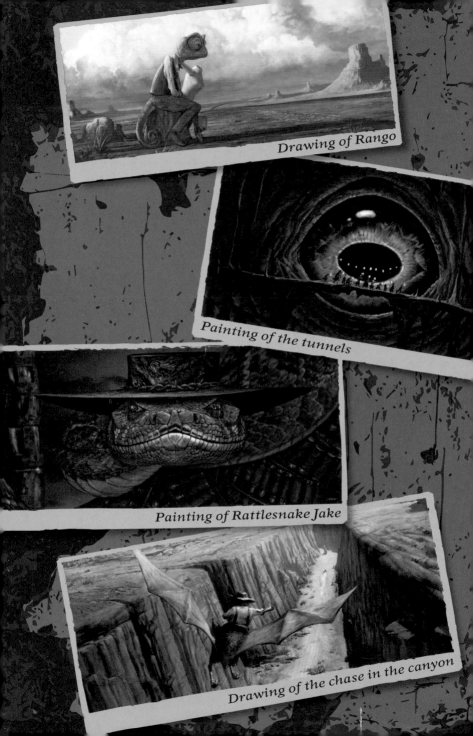

Drawing of Rango

Painting of the tunnels

Painting of Rattlesnake Jake

Drawing of the chase in the canyon

on. You're saying that this jug was empty when you found it?"

Ezekiel nodded. "Uh-huh. That's right!"

Elgin dismissed the prairie dog's statement. "I don't believe a word of it."

"Who would dump water in the desert?" asked Ambrose.

Beans looked at Rango and remembered how they had met. "It wouldn't be the first time," she said.

"It's a puzzle," Waffles agreed.

"What's going on, Sheriff?" Mr. Furgus asked.

"I don't know," Rango admitted, adding, "But I'm going to strip away this mystery and expose its private parts."

Then he told Pappy, "You and your sons are coming with me."

# CHAPTER 9

# THE MAYOR'S GAME

**THE MAIN STREET** clock tower tolled. But this time it did not signal the beginning of the Wednesday water dance. As far as the thirsty townspeople knew, there might never be another Hydration ceremony.

Instead, the clock chimed the hour of the posse's return. All the townspeople looked to the sheriff and his volunteers with hope in their hearts. But one glance at their defeated postures as they rode slowly into Dirt should have told the citizens that the posse had failed.

Still, when everyone saw the prairie dogs in custody, they exclaimed, "Looks like they found the robbers!"

Little Priscilla asked the crucial question, "Where's the water?"

As Beans rode past the dainty mouse she replied, "There's no water."

The terrible news spread swiftly from one dry throat to the next. No water! The posse had returned with three hillbilly prairie dogs and NO WATER!

"Did you hear what she said?" one citizen wondered.

"No water?" another asked, not wanting to believe the truth of their doom.

As Rango approached Priscilla, his heart sank. The little aye-aye looked up at him. Her big eyes were moist with disappointment.

Rango felt completely miserable. He had failed! How could this happen? The hero was never supposed to fail—except maybe to build up dramatic tension before his eventual and inevitable triumph.

Rango had made a solemn promise to a child, a trusting, greedy, bloodthirsty child. And he had broken it.

The chameleon couldn't stand to meet Priscilla's heart-wrenching gaze any longer. He looked at Beans' beautiful eyes to give him the courage to ride ahead to meet his destiny.

"Where's he going?" one of the townspeople wondered as Rango made a slow exit.

Elgin saw the direction that the determined sheriff was riding in. He concluded, "He's going to see the mayor."

Elgin was right. Rango did visit with the mayor, who was playing golf at a nearby pre-construction site. The sheriff wasted no time finding the pit in the desert.

The mayor was golfing with Bad Bill and his gang!

WHACK! Rango heard the smack of a golf club against a sphere balanced on the small, wooden tee.

Rango's brow wrinkled when he recognized the villainous gang, despite their gaudy golf outfits. Their presence confirmed the hero's theory that the mayor was mixed up with this no-good crowd—and just maybe, they were all somehow involved in the scheme to drain Dirt of its water.

As Rango's roadrunner approached the golfers, the mayor's drive sailed high above the lonely pit dotted with construction equipment. The small ball soared to its distant landing . . . and wiggled. The mayor's golf ball was a live pill bug!

The demented rabbit known as Kinski sighed. "Oh, he's gotta be pleased with that swing, yeah?"

"That's a good one, boss!'" Chorizo agreed. The rat did

100

not mind flattering the old tortoise. Soon they would all be rich beyond even Bad Bill's dreams.

The mayor wasn't surprised to see the new sheriff. All the other sheriffs had been suspicious and had come sniffing around for evidence of his wrongdoings. If Rango found out too much, he would simply join the others who were pushing up cacti in Dirt's crowded cemetery.

The old tortoise rolled his wheelchair toward his guest. He told Rango to put on golf shoes before joining him on the course.

As the sheriff changed from cowboy boots to saddle oxfords, he noticed a pair of muddy boots underneath the bench. The large boots were covered with a distinctive reddish-brown mud.

"Huh . . . that's interesting," Rango muttered to himself and filed the information away in the back of his chameleon brain.

The sheriff found the mayor overlooking construction plans with a prairie dog wearing a hard hat. The builder quickly rolled up the plans when Rango approached and left the politician alone with the lawman.

"I do apologize for the shoes, Mr. Rango, but there's

a certain protocol to this game, you understand?" the mayor explained. "I'm a bit of a stickler for protocol."

Rango replied, "Well, that's good. 'Cause you've got a few questions to answer, and I've got my own protocol."

The sheriff's questions made Bill and his men nervous, which made Rango nervous. The only one that didn't break a sweat was the mayor. The old tortoise remained as cold-blooded as his kind.

Rango asked the mayor about the pipe he found in the desert. The clumsy chameleon's clubs suddenly fell out of his bag with a loud CRASH!

Bad Bill argued, "But why would anyone dump water in the bloomin' desert?"

"It seems a bit naïve taking the word of admitted bank robbers, Mr. Rango," the mayor remarked.

Chorizo and Kinski laughed manically.

The sheriff clung to the facts of the case. "But what if somebody did rob the bank before the prairie dogs got there?"

"And who would do that, Mr. Rango?" the mayor retorted. He seemed to have an answer for everything.

The sheriff's eyes narrowed as he drawled, "I was

hoping *you* could tell me." Rango placed one of the pill bugs on the tee while he waited for the mayor's answer.

"That sounds almost like an accusation," the clever tortoise commented casually.

"Take it any way you like," Rango replied in his perfect drawl and assumed a golfer's stance. He swung his club back, keeping a relaxed grip. But the lizard's hold was a little *too* relaxed. Rango's golf club flew out of his hands behind him—and konked Chorizo on the head!

Without missing a beat, Rango continued to question the mayor. "Something you said keeps rattling around in my frontal lobe."

"What's that?" the mayor asked.

"'Control the water and you control everything,'" Rango recited.

The mayor smiled his best sweet and folksy old turtle-who-wouldn't-hurt-a-fly smile. He said smoothly, "Come now, Mr. Rango, do you really think I have divine power? How on earth could I possibly control the water?"

The mayor placed his club on the makeshift green beside his pill bug. Then with patience and precision, he sank his putt with one small swing.

The chameleon completely lacked his opponent's golf skill and experience. Rango wrestled with his clubs and nearly tripped over his own shoes before he finally placed himself in a position to putt.

"You've obviously mastered this game," he acknowledged.

The mayor smiled with false modesty. "Well, I've been playing it for a great many years, sir. I was here before the highway split this great valley. I've watched the march of progress, and I've learned a thing or two. Perhaps it's time you started to take the long view and begin to appreciate the broad sweep of history."

The politician gestured for Rango to look through one of the surveyor's telescopes. Curious, the sheriff put his eye to the scope and saw the town of Dirt.

"Look out there, son. You can almost see time passing," the mayor began grandly.

"What are you building out here?" Rango asked.

"The future, Mr. Rango, the future." The old tortoise's feeble arms tried to embrace the whole vast desert. "One day soon all of this is going to fade into myth. The Frontier Town, the Lawman, the Gunslinger . . . there's just no place for them anymore. We're civilized now.

That's what the future holds. You can either be a part of it or you can be left behind."

As they walked by, Bad Bill and his henchmen heard his remarks. The thugs chuckled.

"Is that what happened to Mr. Merrimack? Did he get left behind?" Rango asked.

"Careful, Mr. Rango," the mayor cautioned. "You seem to forget you're just one little lizard."

In his most dangerous voice, Rango snapped back, "You seem to forget I'm the law around these parts." With that, he turned on his chameleon heels and walked away.

The sheriff was serious. Rango cared about what happened to the folks in this little town, and heroes always made sure justice triumphed over corruption.

As soon as the skinny chameleon was out of earshot, the mayor's slimy smile faded. "Our new sheriff has been playing the hero so long that he's actually starting to believe it. Boys, it's time to call in Rattlesnake Jake."

Bad Bill didn't fear many things. The huge Gila monster had won almost every fight he'd ever been in and he expected that to continue. There was only one creature that made the cruel gang leader wish he could

still run home to his momma. That creature was the meanest, most venomous viper this side of anywhere: Rattlesnake Jake!

To even whisper the serpent's name was enough to bring down a tornado of trouble. Bill shuddered and exclaimed, "What?! Jake's the grim reaper. He never leaves without taking a bloomin' soul!"

"Do it!" the mayor commanded again and hit one final pill bug over the hill. The old tortoise expected to be obeyed. He had big plans for that stretch of sand, bigger plans than all the silver-sucking, gold-grabbing towns in the West put together.

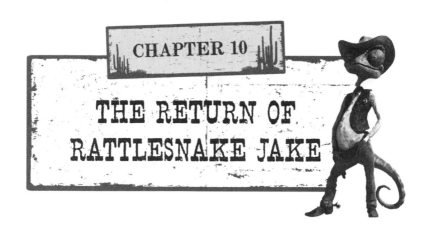

## CHAPTER 10

# THE RETURN OF RATTLESNAKE JAKE

**IN THE SHERIFF'S OFFICE**, Rango, his deputy, and Beans studied a map of Dirt and the surrounding desert.

Wounded Bird observed, "The mayor has bought up all the land in the valley, except your ranch, Miss Beans."

Beans shook her head. "It just doesn't make sense. Without water, that land is useless."

"Unless you control the water," Rango mused. "If he controlled the water, the mayor could turn it back on once he bought up all the land."

"But how could he control the water?" Beans wondered.

Before Rango could invent a plausible answer, little Priscilla ran in from the street and announced, "Sheriff, we got a problem."

Priscilla's "problem" was actually a riot! The moment Rango opened the door, he heard the loud, angry shouts of a mob.

Rango held up both hands and addressed the crowd in his manliest drawl, "Hold on! Calm down everyone. Let me talk!"

The crowd roared. They didn't want talk.

Bonnie accused Rango, "You said you'd bring back the water."

Buford didn't know what to think any more. "It's just . . . we got no hope without that water," he told the sheriff.

"We got nothing left to believe in," Spoons added.

Rango knew the townsfolk needed someone or something to trust. This was the part in the story where the hero made a rousing speech that helped everyone pull together instead of falling apart.

The chameleon pointed to the sign above and said, "You see that sign up there? As long as that sign says SHERIFF, you can believe that there's law and order in this town. You want something to believe in, Spoons? Believe in me. Believe in that there sign. As long as it hangs there, we've got hope."

BANG! BANG! BANG! BANG! BANG! BANG! The sheriff sign bounced to the ground. Everyone spun around and heard a loud RRRRRAAAAATTTTTLLLLLLEEEEE!

The crowd stepped back in terror as the villainous creature slithered closer.

The cosseted chameleon had never even imagined such a creature. Blood-red hues flickered like flames in the viper's shiny, black eyes as he hissed, "Hello, brother."

The snake drained some venom into a cup and presented it to Rango. "Thirsty?"

Rattlesnake Jake chuckled as he slid sideways toward the trembling townsfolk. The snake's oozing, curling coils seemed to hypnotize everyone except the mayor, Bad Bill, and his gang.

The Gila monster had the mayor's assurance that Jake was here to "tango with Rango," and he hoped the snake wouldn't kill the skinny lizard too quickly. Out this far in the desert, live entertainment was a rare treat.

Jake slowly circled around the sheriff. Jake's flat head oscillated back and forth under the brim of his black hat, like a watch dangled from a hypnotist's hand. The

menacing snake hissed, "It'sss been a long time, brother. How have you been keeping?"

Rango stalled, "Oh, well, you know . . ."

Suddenly Jake's forked tongue flicked out with a loud HISSS!

The sheriff's ten-gallon hat blew right off his head. The chameleon froze. That hat was an important part of his costume. Without it, Rango felt even less like a hero.

"I hear you've been telling everyone about how you killed all them Jenkinsss brothers."

Rango felt too terrified to move.

The snake continued, "All thessse good folks here believe your little ssstoriesss, don't they?"

He slid over to Priscilla and Beans. The little mouse's huge eyes widened even more with fear as Jake hissed on, "Ssseemsss thessse folksss trussst you. They think you're gonna sssave their little town."

Rango felt ashamed for being afraid and helpless, but also for all the lies he had so happily told to puff up his image.

The snake sneered on, "They think you're gonna sssave their little sssoulsss. But we know better, don't we?"

Jake coiled himself slickly around Beans. She squirmed in his dangerous embrace.

Rango suffered a mix of miserable emotions. What could one small chameleon do against such a powerful enemy? Rango stood frozen, as still as Beans during one of her spells.

Rattlesnake Jake challenged the sheriff. "Ssso why don't you show your friendsss here what you're made of? Ssshow 'em who you really are."

The cornered chameleon could no longer hide his fear. Rango shook from head to toe.

Jake enjoyed seeing the bragging coward reveal his true colors. The reptile looked deep into Rango's eyes and sneered, "You didn't do any of the thingsss you sssaid, did you? You didn't kill them Jenkinsss brothers. You're not even from the Wessst, are you?"

Rango mumbled miserably, "No."

"Oh, ssspeak up!" Jake exclaimed impatiently. "I don't think your friendsss heard you."

Rango made his confession a bit louder. "No."

"All you've done isss lie to the thessse good people. You're nothing but a fake and a coward, isssn't that right?" Rattlesnake Jake insisted.

111

"Yes," Rango agreed.

"Louder!" Rattlesnake Jake shook his tail for emphasis.

"Yes!" Rango cried in utter humiliation and fear.

Jake circled the little lizard, coiling ominously. "Lisssten closse, you pathetic fraud. Thisss isss my town now!"

The snake uncoiled and oozed against Rango, pushing him forward. The crowd backed away, averting their eyes from the disgraced sheriff's gaze. Only Priscilla looked up at Rango hopefully. Her oversized eyes seemed to beg, "Say it's not so!"

Rango shuffled on to Beans. But he couldn't bring himself to even look her.

Beans was disgusted by his deception. Tears clouded her beautiful eyes as she asked, "Who are you?"

The question hung unanswered in the dusty air.

Rango just kept shuffling one heavy foot in front of the other until he reached the edge of town. The blinding desert day gave way to purple evening as Rango stopped in front of the cemetery. The tombstones of previous sheriffs reminded the chameleon that things could be worse—but not by much.

Rango removed the shiny sheriff's star that had once made him so happy. He studied the metal symbol of justice, law, courage, and duty. Feeling like a complete failure, the lizard let it slide through his fingers into the dust.

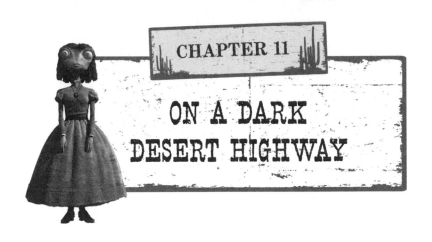

# CHAPTER 11

## ON A DARK DESERT HIGHWAY

**RANGO FAILED TO NOTICE** the dazzling blanket of stars twinkling across the desert sky. The theatrical chameleon no longer cared about beauty or anything else, not even whether he lived or died.

Somehow his feet found their way back to the highway where his miserable adventure began.

VROOOM! A car rushed by, headlights briefly illuminating the desert and the lonely road. Rango saw something familiar up ahead. It was his old windup fish, Mr. Timms!

He picked up the plastic fish and hugged his old friend. Then Rango spotted his headless costar and hurried to her side. With his arm around his stage girlfriend, the chameleon sighed. Then he sadly repeated and answered Beans' parting question, "Who am I? I am nobody."

Rango sat by the side of the highway feeling lower than a pimple on a fat dog's belly. Another car ZOOMED past, making the darkness seem all the blacker as its taillights disappeared into the distance.

Without giving it a second thought, Rango started to walk across the highway. He knew from his adventure with Roadkill that he might get squashed. He half hoped one of the WHOOSHING cars would put him out of his misery.

Several came close enough to ruffle his neckerchief in their wakes. But they did not crush him.

Rango reached the other side of the road in even deeper despair. The klutzy chameleon couldn't even get run over!

Rango collapsed, too tired and miserable to do anything but sleep.

During the night the desert became a whole new world. Day creatures scurried to their nests and burrows, and the night dwellers emerged to explore their cool, colorless realm.

Those who believe in things like Walking Cacti might say the refreshing night wind also brought a certain magic to the lonely dunes.

Perhaps roused by some magic wind, pill bugs uncurled all around the has-been hero as he snored. The strange little bugs slipped under the chameleon and, like a living magic carpet, carried him over the starlit sands to meet his destiny.

Well after dawn, Rango opened his eyes to the blinding sun. He squinted, confused. Where was the highway? And what was that big white thing?

Rango thought mirages looked like water—not golf carts! The curious chameleon took a closer look at the cart. It contained all sorts of things, including four golden statuettes.

Rango shivered with an eerie realization. He muttered to himself, amazed, "The Golden Guardians. The Alabaster Carriage."

It was just as Roadkill had described! Then Rango saw the silhouette of a tall, thin man. Rango immediately recognized his squinty eyes and weathered face. The awed actor breathed, "The Spirit of the West!"

Rango heard a humming noise and noticed the man was sweeping a metal detector over the sand. After a few seconds, Rango worked up the courage to speak to him.

"Um . . . excuse me! Mr. Spirit, sir," he began.

Having finally detected some metal, the thin man picked up an old fishing hook and tucked it in his pocket.

"Ahh! There's a beauty," he remarked, adding, "Sometimes you gotta dig deep to find what you're looking for. So . . . you made it."

Rango suddenly felt confused. "Is this heaven?"

The Spirit of the West shook his head. A sliver of a smile flitted across his face.

Rango couldn't understand why someone so great would be digging around in the desert. "What are you doing out here?"

"Searching. Same as you," the Spirit replied.

Rango sighed. "I don't even know what I'm looking for anymore. I don't even know who I am."

The tall man's eyes squinted in the far distance. "These days they got a name for just about everything. Lemme tell you one thing. It doesn't matter what they call you. It's the deeds that make the man."

Rango sighed again. "My deeds just made things worse. I'm a fraud, a phony. My friends believed in me, but they need some kind of hero."

"Then be a hero," the Spirit suggested simply.

"Oh, no. No, I . . ." Rango objected. "You don't understand. I'm not even supposed to be here."

The Spirit of the West nodded. "That's right. You came a long way to find something that isn't out there. Don't you see? It's not about you. It's about them."

Rango thought about how much the poor, dry Dirtonians must hate him now! The chameleon shook his head. "But I can't go back."

The Spirit climbed into his golf cart. "Don't know that you got a choice, son." His intense eyes peered at Rango through the windshield. One thin finger drew a little box around Rango on the dusty plastic. The rectangle reminded Rango of the frame he had drawn on his breath-fogged terrarium glass.

"No man can walk out on his own story," the Spirit of the West concluded. Then the golf cart commenced its slow progress across the sand.

The lizard felt totally alone until a voice nearby piped up, "Makes you think, doesn't it?"

Rango turned and saw Roadkill! One glance at the armadillo's gently radiant smile told Rango that his old amigo had found inner peace.

Roadkill nodded. "That's right, amigo. That was the Spirit of the West."

Rango would've figured Roadkill for crow's food long ago. Yet there he was, smiling.

"So you made it to the other side of the road," Rango marveled.

Roadkill smiled. "Mmhmm. Beautiful, isn't it?"

The two shared a quiet moment. Rango sighed, surprised to feel happiness again. "Yeah, it is."

"Come, my friend," the contented armadillo said. "I want to show you something."

Roadkill led Rango to a fish skeleton that was partially fossilized by the searing heat. Nearby, he noticed an enormous decaying boat hull. Rango wondered what fish bones and a boat were doing out in the desert?

"Many years ago this entire valley was covered in aqua. Now, only one question remains," Roadkill stated.

Rango answered, "Where did it go?"

Out of the corner of his eye, Rango thought he glimpsed something moving. The chameleon turned and saw cacti in the distance. He stared at the plants, stunned to discover that they were walking!

The needle-covered plants slowly dragged themselves by their roots across the sand. Rango recalled Beans' curious legend.

"They follow the water," he remarked with growing excitement. "They follow the water! Come on!"

Rango followed the line of Walking Cacti up a hill. At the top, he and Roadkill saw a huge water pipe running along the hill leading to the sparkling city of Las Vegas. It looked like something straight out of a movie. But even more dazzling to the lizard than Las Vegas' neon lights were the many fountains, pools, and sprinklers spraying water everywhere! If only some of this water could find its way back to Dirt . . .

# CHAPTER 12

# FOUNTAINS IN THE DESERT

**THE WATER GUSHING** all over Las Vegas reminded Rango of his first morning in the desert, when he fell out of the pipe at Beans' feet. He also recalled the muddy boots he'd spotted at the mayor's construction site, and Beans bemoaning, "It just don't make sense."

Memories raced through Rango's mind: Merrimack's glasses in the empty water bottle and the map of the desert he had studied with Beans and Deputy Wounded Bird.

Rango remembered Beans' words: "Without water that land is useless."

Rango shuddered at the next memory, the one he wished he could erase forever. In dreadful detail, Rango recalled Rattlesnake Jake holding Beans in his coils.

Rango pushed the awful thought away and

remembered the mayor golfing at his construction site. "What are you building out here?" Rango had asked.

"The future, Mr. Rango, the future," the politician had replied.

Rango walked over to the big pipe. He spoke the mayor's fateful statement, "Control the water and you control everything." He remembered the politician evading his accusation at the bank vault and how the mayor had protested, "How on earth could I possibly control the water?"

Rango followed the freaky line of moving cacti up to a strange circle as mysterious and solemn as the giant rocks arranged at Stonehenge. As he walked nearer, Rango finally saw the object at the center of the slow cacti circle. It was a water valve! At the bottom it read: EMERGENCY SHUT-OFF VALVE #6.

Rango immediately recognized some of Bad Bill's red-mud boot prints around the huge valve.

For a long moment, the chameleon froze as these facts sank in and their implications swiftly multiplied. Suddenly, all the pieces fit together. The mayor was buying up "useless" land to build more cities like Las Vegas.

Rango looked back toward Dirt.

"What now, amigo?" Roadkill wondered.

Rango's eyes squinted with steely determination, like those of his hero. The lizard repeated, "No man can walk out on his own story." Then he added, "I'm going back."

"But why?" the armadillo asked.

Rango suddenly had the answer to the question that had troubled him all his life. "Because that's who I am."

Before he faced Rattlesnake Jake again, the clever chameleon came up with a plan. Rango knew he could never defeat the giant snake alone. But he also knew a whole town full of feisty fighters who had good reason to help him.

Rango soon reached the narrow canyon leading to the prairie dog town. He did not expect a warm welcome. After all, he had arrested their beloved leader.

But the fast-talking lizard hoped he could persuade the varmints to see the advantage of working together. Almost as soon as Rango stepped near the hole-dotted cliffs, Maybelle appeared, stomping toward him on her single boot.

"You've got a lot of nerve showing up here, lawman. What is it you want?" the ornery rodent demanded.

"Your pappy and them boys are in jail for something they didn't do," Rango began. "But I've got a plan."

## CHAPTER 13

## THE DUEL FOR DIRT

**THE CHAMELEON'S PLAN** included stopping at the cemetery to retrieve a certain piece of symbolic jewelry. Wind swirled through the graveyard, drifting between the tombstones of sheriffs past.

Rango saw his silver star glinting in the dust. He picked it up and pinned it back on. The sheriff's chest might not have been impressively broad, but the look in his eyes was as determined as any true hero's.

As Rango was swaggering back into town, the mayor poured Beans a glass of water. Bad Bill and his gang sprawled on the sofa in the mayor's office, wearing clothes and hats more suited to businessmen than thugs. Rattlesnake Jake coiled in a corner, ready to strike on command.

The politician oozed sympathy while the thirsty

cowgirl considered both the water and the deed to her daddy's ranch spread out on the mayor's desk.

"I appreciate how difficult this is for you, Beans. But you're making a practical decision."

"Decisssionsss, decisssionsss," Jake hissed.

"There's no need for anymore suffering," the mayor stated. Then he slurped some water from his own glass. Extremely tempted, the dry-throated lizard grabbed her glass.

"Your family's ranch is nothing but a wasteland now. Sign the deed," the mayor said, sliding the papers closer to Beans. "And relieve yourself of your father's burden."

At the mention of her beloved father, Beans snapped out of her thirsty trance.

"My daddy was not a burden!" she declared defiantly, splashing the mayor with her glass of water. "Keep your blood money and I'll keep my land."

Without any warning, Rattlesnake Jake wrapped himself around Beans' chair. The snake's head performed a dangerous sideways dance. Bad Bill's gang laughed at the girl's distress.

The snake threatened, "Do what he sssaysss or by all

126

the firesss of the black pit, I'll sssqueeze them pretty blue eyesss out of your ssskull."

Under the intense pressure from Jake's tightening coils, Beans' chair started to crack and break.

At these ominous sounds, all laughter left the room. Not even the mayor meant for Jake to squash Miss Beans like a frijole! He protested, "Hold on, now, Jake. There's no need for—"

To everyone's shock, Jake swiftly turned on the mayor, hissing, "Let me do my job! You brought me in and now we're gonna play thisss out until the end."

He spun his head back to Beans while his coils crushed her chair. "Sssign the paper."

"No!" Beans replied hotly.

Jake jerked the cowgirl close, forcing her to look him right in the eyes as he choked her. The black pits bored into Beans' beautiful eyes.

Then from the street below, everyone in the mayor's office heard shouting.

"JAAAKE, I'M CALLING YOU OUT!"

The startled snake spun around and looked out the window. It was an image straight out of a classic Western movie. The hero was risking everything to bring the

villain to justice. In this case, that hero was a skinny chameleon known as Rango.

Rattlesnake Jake smiled. "Thisss day jussst got a little more interesssting."

Rango continued to swagger toward his destiny. Awestruck townspeople gathered to catch a glimpse of their savior returned.

Jake slammed out of the mayor's office, taking Beans with him. When she saw Rango, she couldn't believe her eyes. Her hero had come back just in the nick of time!

"Put her down," Rango commanded.

Amused, Jake asked, "Or what, little man? You gonna ssshoot me?"

This time, Rango wasn't afraid. "That's just about the size of it."

The new cool conviction in Rango's voice surprised Jake. He tossed Beans to Bad Bill's gang.

The cowgirl protested, "Get your filthy paws off me!"

Bad Bill stuffed a gag in her mouth.

Jake hissed, "Alright, Sssheriff. Make your move."

Rango and the rattlesnake took positions for a showdown in the center of town.

High above both hero and villain, the town clock ticked toward high noon. The wind died down and the still air hung above Main Street as if it, too, was waiting to watch the duel.

The townsfolk scrambled away from the street, hiding behind closed doors and shutters, peering through windows and cracks to glimpse the deadly duel.

BONG! The clock tolled the first of twelve chimes. BONG!

Rango and Jake slowly moved toward each other, step by slither by step. Beans could hardly bear to watch. How could her hero possibly hope to defeat this mighty adversary?

BONG! BONG!

Hero and villain stepped and slithered closer. Under the pitiless noonday sun, Jake rattled ominously. Rango's eyes narrowed and the chameleon's tongue flicked out to eat a bug.

Wounded Bird moved toward the top of the clock tower. The loyal deputy was armed.

Rango and Jake moved even closer.

BONG! BONG!

Rango looked up at the town's tall clock. It clicked

to a minute past noon. Main Street fell silent.

On a nearby hilltop, the sun passed Roadkill's staff. The enlightened armadillo cried, "Now, amigo!"

The cactus spirits surrounding EMERGENCY SHUT-OFF VALVE #6 started slowly turning the valve with ropes.

Underground, rodents chanted, "Heave! Heave!" as they pulled down a section of pipe with more ropes— just as Rango had planned.

As Rango and Jake drew closer together, the huge snake stood over the prairie dog's newly repaired hole in front of the bank.

High above, Wounded Bird took aim at the villainous, venomous reptile. Then suddenly Jake spun around and fired, knocking Wounded Bird off the tower. The deputy crashed into the building next door.

Little Priscilla rushed to see if Wounded Bird was okay.

The deputy said simply, "That was a bad idea."

Jake turned back to Rango, sliding back into position over the patched hole. Satisfied that the snake was in the right spot once more, Rango asked, "Thirsty, brother?"

Rango smiled and Jake suddenly suspected that something was wrong. In the tunnels below Dirt, a

130

rumbling sound preceded the welcome GUSH of water cascading through the pipe.

The rodents shouted, "Here it comes!"

WHOOSH! Water rushed up toward Main Street.

Jake felt the vibrations below and exclaimed in confusion, "What? No!"

A geyser of water exploded under the snake, sending him spinning and writhing high up into the air.

Spoons shouted, "It's a miracle!"

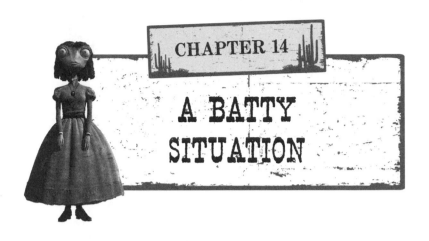

# CHAPTER 14

# A BATTY SITUATION

**MORE JETS OF WATER** shot up all over town as bystanders scrambled to safety from the rushing tides.

From the jail, Pappy, Ezekiel, and Jedidiah watched in amazement.

"Look at that!" Jedidiah shouted.

"What is that?!" asked Pappy since he couldn't see what was happening.

Suddenly, a geyser broke through the jail's floor and out through the ceiling.

"That's our salvation, Pa!" Ezekiel answered.

Pappy grinned, "It's a jail break, boys. We're bustin' out!" He clutched his sons as the three prairie dogs rode the gushing geysers to freedom.

A short distance up Main Street another column of water shot through the clock tower, completely

destroying the landmark. Rattlesnake Jake finally obeyed one law—the law of gravity. The heavy snake landed with a loud THUD.

He turned to the sheriff, hissing with hate, "I'm gonna blow ssso many holesss in you, your gutsss will be leakin' lead!"

Cool as a cucumber, Rango replied, "Well, then, it's a good thing I brought some backup."

The sky above Main Street suddenly darkened, shadowed by the huge silhouette of a swooping hawk!

Jake recoiled in terror, slinking back, away from the big bird. But as the frightened reptile watched, part of the bird seemed to break off and then rejoin the main body. Jake stared closer, gradually realizing it wasn't a hawk. It was a swarm of bats!

Furious and no longer afraid, Rattlesnake Jake roared as he took aim on the skies. BLAM! BLAM! BLAM! BLAM!

Leading the squadron, Maybelle cried, "Break formation, children!"

Jake laughed, truly enjoying the battle.

The bats swooped away to safety just as Jake ran out of ammunition.

Rango stood his ground in front of the serpent.

Jake's black eyes blinked. He knew that look. He *was* that look. The snake realized he could not beat that look. He sank into his coils, defeated.

Then the mayor shouted, "Oh, Mr. Rango! Aren't you forgetting something?"

Rango turned and saw the mayor sitting in his wheelchair beside Bad Bill, who had Beans in his grasp. Stump and Kinski laughed as they escorted the captive girl into the bank.

For a moment no one moved, including Rango. What would happen to his beloved Beans? No, Rango couldn't risk her life. He surrendered and swaggered into the bank.

Bad Bill and his boys laughed as they threw Rango and Beans into the vault. They closed the round glass door and locked it. Almost instantly, water rushed up from the hole in the floor.

The mayor laughed as Rango and Beans stumbled in the churning, rising waters. Rango reassured his sweetheart, "Beans, hold on! Don't worry. I've got a plan."

He turned to the glass vault door and shouted,

"HELP!" The chameleon pounded on the thick glass and cried, "OPEN THE DOOR!"

But, of course, the villains did nothing to save the helpless hero and the increasingly damp cowgirl. The chameleon sighed, "Okay. Plan B."

Beans tried to talk through her gag.

Rango exclaimed, "What? Beans, you're mumbling."

The water kept rising!

Beyond the glass door, the mayor and his henchmen enjoyed the show. The politician savored this satisfying moment.

"All my problems taken care of, except for one," he said and turned his weapon on Rattlesnake Jake. The snake was shocked!

The mayor stated, "It's a new West, Jake. There's no place for you anymore. We're businessmen now. You and the sheriff are more alike than you think. You're nothing but legends. Pretty soon no one will believe you even existed."

Kinski tipped his fancy chapeau. "We got new hats!"

Inside the vault, the waters rose even higher. But all was not lost. Rango opened his hand to reveal a single, shiny bullet. He gingerly placed the bullet in his

mouth between his teeth to free his hands and remove Beans' gag.

As soon as she was free to speak, Beans gushed, "You came back!" She was so happy to see her hero that she completely forgot about being shy and gave Rango a huge kiss . . . and then coughed as the bullet traveled down her throat!

"No need to panic," said Rango who was still swooning from the kiss, "but I think you just swallowed Plan B."

Rango wrapped his arms around Beans and performed the Heimlich Maneuver, squeezing until the bullet shot from her mouth.

BANG! The bullet struck the vault door. Instantly, a spider web of cracks appeared on the glass. The mayor had just enough time to realize what had happened before . . .

CRASH! WHOOSH! The door collapsed completely under the weight of a rushing wave! The water slammed Bad Bill and his boys against one wall and sent Jake smashing out the bank's front windows, floating up onto Main Street.

Rango and Beans tumbled around, as helpless as

socks in a washing machine. But eventually they wound up wet and gasping for air on Main Street along with the mayor.

Rango helped Beans to her feet. He looked down at the mayor who floated helplessly on his shell. Though his wheelchair was still in the bank and he couldn't even flip over, the mayor did not give up. Instead, he tried to negotiate.

"Now, Sheriff, I'm sure if we work together, we can reach a mutually beneficial solution to our current unfortunate situation . . ."

Rango looked past the helpless tortoise as he remarked, "You'd better take it up with him."

Rango kicked the mayor's shell, spinning him toward Rattlesnake Jake!

Something glinting in the water momentarily distracted the reptile. Jake saw Rango's lonely bullet floating down the street.

The snake turned to Rango and remarked, "I tip my hat to you, from one legend to another."

Rango returned the gesture, acknowledging Jake's show of respect.

The rattlesnake turned back to the mayor and asked,

"What was that you said? Pretty soon no one will believe you even existed."

Before the fast-talking tortoise had time to reply, Jake struck! His powerful coils quickly encircled the mayor, who cried, "Whoa! Jake, no-nooOOOO!"

But the snake only squeezed tighter and tugged the mayor down the street toward the empty desert and his doom.

As Rango and Beans watched, the snake and his unwilling cargo gradually vanished, hidden behind heat ripples rising off the smoldering sands.

# CHAPTER 15

# WELCOME TO MUD

**NOW THAT THE DANGER** of drought, the mayor, and Rattlesnake Jake were gone, the townsfolk came out of hiding. They splashed joyously in the newfound floodwaters.

Little Priscilla ran toward Rango, eager to embrace the hero. "Rango! You brought back the water just like you promised." The small girl hugged the sheriff tightly and spoke the phrase he had longed to hear all his life. "You really are a hero."

Rango chuckled, kneeling down to the child. "Well, the thing about heroes is, whenever you—"

Priscilla put her hands up to stop the lizard from lecturing. "Don't spoil it."

Rango nodded. "Right."

All around the happy hero, damp Dirtonians laughed

and splashed and cheered. Rango took Beans by the hand and smiled, saying, "Well, I don't know about you, but I could sure go for a dip."

Perched from a rooftop, the owl mariachis played festive tunes to accompany the joyful celebration.

"And so the lizard completes his journey from humble beginnings to the legend we sing of today," remarked Señor Flan. "And although he is certain to die—perhaps from a household accident, which accounts for sixty-five percent of all unnatural deaths—the people of the village will honor his memory, even as they abandon their dignity."

Dirt remained a happy town, although some things did change. For one, there was so much water that the town couldn't be called Dirt anymore. By official proclamation and unanimous decision, the town's name was changed to Mud.

The critters enjoyed new pastimes, such as relaxing on beach chairs between dips in the town's generous supply of cool, clear water.

Angelique, Melonee, and her friend Fresca opened a Bath Stand. They charged real money instead of water. When Turley tried to pay for a bath with a

jug, Fresca replied, "Water's not money. Money is money now."

It seemed the only problem the little town had was keeping Mr. Snuggles out of the wading pool. The poor porcupine just couldn't get used to the idea that sharp quills and inflatable pools can't be friends.

Perhaps inspired by the sheriff's sweet romance with Beans, Waffles began courting the headless doll. The twitchy toad cozied up to her and cooed, "I really think you complete me."

The prairie dogs gave up stealing in favor of theater. Pappy, Ezekiel, and Jedidiah even practiced their own stage play under Ezekiel's direction. The prairie dog looked quite dashing with his cap and megaphone.

Pappy recited, "Prithee unhand my fair maiden."

Ezekiel cried, "Cut! Cut! Everybody take five . . ."

Jedidiah complained, "Pappy, you keep missing your mark."

The blind, old prairie dog wondered, "What's my motivation?"

Nearby, the neighborhood kids buried Doc up to his head in sand. Then they dumped a bucket of pill bugs on him. Doc chuckled, "Oh, you kids!"

Priscilla poked Doc with a stick. The rabbit cried, "OW! Now what did you do that for?"

Priscilla replied, "I was just checkin'. I hear if you get too sunburned you can peel a man's face right off."

Wounded Bird sat on the lifeguard tower with a megaphone. The deputy announced, "Adult swim. Next five minutes. Stay between the buoys!"

Rango might have enjoyed swimming, but the sheriff had more important things to do. He sat astride his roadrunner, surrounded by a growing crowd of adoring Mudtonians.

Beans handed her hero a paper bag. "Now I packed your lunch. You've got a danish, and I picked out the raisins, just like you like it."

Rango muttered under his breath, "Beans!"

But she rattled on anyway, "Don't forget your nasal spray is in your saddle bag."

"Beans!" the embarrassed sheriff tried again.

But the pretty cowgirl couldn't help it. She loved him so! "And your moisturizing lotion is—"

Rango whispered, "Now, Beans, we talked about this."

Ambrose asked, "Sheriff, where are you headed?"

"Oh, well, there's trouble down Dry Creek. Bad Bill's been acting up again," Rango replied.

Beans fretted, "Now, honey, you come back with all your digits. Don't go trying to be a hero."

Rango muttered. "Beans, you're missing the point. I've got an image to protect now." Then the sheriff exclaimed, "Whoa! Where are my Tic Tacs?!"

A rattling sound startled the crowd. But it wasn't the return of the dreaded snake. The sheriff had found his breath mints.

Rango turned his roadrunner toward the horizon. Then he rode off to his next adventure!

Beans waved and smiled. She had finally found the place she'd always dreamed of as a child, someplace wonderful with plenty of water. Strangely enough, it was the very same town—plus one hero.

When Rango rode past Roadkill and the slow-moving cactus spirits, the armadillo exclaimed, "Give them a good one, amigo."

The sheriff continued up the side of a mesa where he prepared to address the town. Rango struggled to steady his lively bird. "Are you ready, Excelsior?"

The roadrunner stomped one foot, and the sheriff

began, "My fellow comrades! There will be times when you doubt yourself, when you feel pummeled by the cataclysms of life. Remember this moment. Remember me. Know that I will be there watching you . . . sometimes at inappropriate moments. That's part of the deal. And remember that within all of us resides the true spirit of the wh . . . whoa—WHOA!"

Tired of speeches, Excelsior suddenly reared up, nearly tipping Rango right out of the saddle. The long-winded chameleon squeezed his knees to keep from falling, and then suggested, "Let's take it from the top."